The Secret of the Hidden Tunnel

© Day One Publications 2012

First printed 2012

ISBN 978-1-84625-334-8

All Scripture quotations are from the **New International Version** 1984
Copyright © 1973, 1978, 1984

Published by Day One Publications
Ryelands Road, Leominster, HR6 8NZ

TEL 01568 613 740 FAX 01568 611 473

email—sales@dayone.co.uk

UK web site—www.dayone.co.uk

USA web site—www.dayonebookstore.com

Designed by **documen**
Printed by 4edge Limited, UK

Dedication

To my great-niece, Anna.
May you grow to love and follow the
Lord Jesus more and more

My grateful thanks go to my ever-patient husband, Malcolm, who graciously allows me to spend hours in the study and always encourages me. My thanks also go to Tirzah Jones, the team at Day One, and Suzanne Mitchell. Thank you for having faith in me.

1 The news

Matilda Morris, or Matty, as she was usually called, had just celebrated her eleventh birthday. Everything in her world seemed wonderful. She was in her last year of primary school and had just been chosen for the school netball team. She loved her lessons, loved sport and had lots of friends. Although she had no brothers or sisters, she knew her parents loved her and she was very happy. That was, until the day she heard the news!

Matty had an idea that something was going on at home. Her mum and dad seemed to be talking loudly and arguing with each other, but as soon as she appeared, they shut up or changed the conversation. There was definitely 'an atmosphere' in the house.

One evening, just after the family had eaten their evening meal, her father cleared his throat. 'Matty,' he said, 'Mummy and I have something we want to tell you. I have to go away with my work. Usually, as you know, I only go for a few weeks, but this time I'm afraid it's for two years.'

'Oh Daddy!' interrupted Matty. 'That's such a long time! We'll miss you so much! But I promise I'll be good and will look after Mummy,' she added.

'I'm afraid, sweetheart, it isn't as simple as that,' replied her dad. 'This time Mummy will be coming with me. But where we're going isn't really suitable for you to go to school, so we've decided that you should go to a boarding school here and then come and be with us in the holidays.'

For once, Matty was speechless. She just looked from her mum to her dad, her eyes filling with tears. She felt the anger beginning to well up inside her and she wanted to scream at them both, 'I won't go there, I hate you!' Instead, she ran out of the room, slamming the door behind her, and stormed up to her bedroom. She flung herself onto her bed and began to sob. 'It isn't fair!' she told herself. 'Why do I have to go away to a boarding school? I want to go to Springhead High along with all my friends.'

After a few minutes there was a tap at her door. 'Matty, please let me come in and talk to you,' she heard her mum say. Matty grunted a miserable 'OK'.

Her mother came and sat on the end of her bed. 'I know you're very upset just now, but please listen to me,' she said. 'Daddy is going to work in Africa for a couple of years. He is going to a country called Burundi and I will go with him. Burundi has been through a difficult time with a long civil war. There really isn't a suitable school for you there. We've been thinking about it for weeks now, because you're so special to us and we hate to leave you behind, but we have to do what is best for you. You'll be able to come out in the school holidays and be with us then. The school we've chosen is really nice and I'm going to take you there to see it next week.'

'But why can't I stay with one of my friends and go to Springhead High like everyone else?' sobbed Matty. 'I don't want to go to a boarding school—I want to go to Africa with you!'

'If it was just for a few weeks, I'm sure that you could stay with a friend, but two years is a long time. I know you'll soon make friends and even find that boarding school is great fun!' Her mum tried to cheer her up.

So the following week, a very disgruntled Matty went with her parents to see her new school. It was situated near the sea, on the edge of a town. The building looked rather old and a bit like a church. Matty didn't like the look of it at all. Inside, it seemed even worse. There were so many corridors that she was sure she would get lost. The headmistress welcomed them and showed them around the school, the boarding houses and the gardens. Matty cheered up a bit when she saw the gardens. They were large and had lots of places where she could hide. One of her favourite games was hide-and-seek.

They were invited to have lunch in the school dining room, or 'refectory', as the headmistress called it. She was a middle-aged lady with grey hair neatly tied back, and she seemed kind; when she smiled her eyes crinkled up, which Matty liked. Quite a lot of the teachers were young and friendly. Matty looked at the girls, who ranged from about eight years old to eighteen. At least they all looked cheerful and were chatting together. Maybe it wouldn't be so horrible after all. The headmistress introduced Matty and her parents to the class teacher of Year 7, which she would enter next term. 'You'll be in a class of about sixteen girls,' the headmistress said. 'At the moment, we think that six of you will be boarders.'

'Only sixteen!' Matty was amazed. 'There are twenty-nine in my class now, and twenty-eight in the other Year 6 class!' she told the teacher.

'We like to have small classes so that we can get to know you all well,' the headmistress replied. 'We like school to be a family, especially for our boarders. I'm sure you will like it here at St Anne's.'

'St Anne's!' Matty thought to herself. 'How my friends are going to laugh at me when I tell them the name of my new school sounds like a church, and also when they see the posh uniform I have to wear!' She still wished she could go to Springhead High with all her friends from primary school, but she knew her parents had made up their minds and there really was no choice. But her visit to the school had made her feel a bit happier. Everyone had seemed very friendly.

It was horrible at the end of term when she had to say goodbye to all her friends. She told them as little as possible about her new school. That summer holiday wasn't much fun, either. Usually the family went to the seaside and had a great time together, but this year they couldn't. They were too busy shopping for all the things that she would need for school and that her parents needed for Burundi. Her dad and mum were very busy preparing to go to Africa. It seemed to Matty that they didn't even notice how miserable she sometimes felt and how much she was dreading leaving home. The family made a few trips to visit relatives to say goodbye, but there was no one she could talk to and tell what she was really feeling.

Eventually, the dreaded day arrived when she packed her trunk, put on her new uniform and was driven by her parents to St Anne's School. Many other girls were arriving at the same time and they all seemed to know one another. Matty felt lost and lonely. A very small lady who appeared to be rather old took Matty and her parents down one of the long, dark corridors and into her boarding house. They were led to a dormitory which had three bunk beds in it.

'This is your dorm,' the lady said to Matty. 'I will be your housemistress—my name is Miss Grace. You're the first pupil from Year 7 to arrive, so you can choose which bed you would like. You can choose a wardrobe, too, and put your things away. The porter will bring your trunk up in just a few minutes.'

Matty tried to swallow hard so that she didn't cry. 'Thank you,' she managed to whisper to Miss Grace, who quickly disappeared to help another girl find her room. Matty decided to have a top bunk that was near a window, so that she could see into the garden below. Her dad gave her hand a squeeze. 'If you really hate it here, you must tell us and we'll find somewhere else for you. I've got a present for you—a mobile phone that will let you to talk to us in Burundi. The headmistress will allow you to do that in your free time, and we've given her some pocket money for you which you can use to pay for it. We want to hear from our daughter at least once a week!'

Matty looked at her parents, and for the first time she realized they were also trying not to cry and this was very hard for them too. She tried to smile and be enthusiastic about the phone. 'Thank you so much!' she said. 'I'm so glad I'll be able to talk to you!'

'Just promise to tell us if you hate it here, and about any worries or problems you might have,' repeated Matty's dad.

2 Sandy

The door opened again and in ran a girl with a long ginger ponytail and freckles all over her face.

'Hi!' she said to Matty. 'I'm Beatrice Sandra Jane Thompson, but everyone calls me Sandy. You're new, aren't you? What's your name?'

'I'm Matilda Morris, but everyone calls me Matty,' Matty replied.

'Have you chosen a bed yet?' Sandy asked. Matty pointed up to the bunk she wanted.

'Can I sleep under you? I think we'll be great friends!' Sandy said.

The two girls smiled at each other, liking what they saw and instantly knowing that they would indeed be very good friends. Matty's parents also smiled, full of relief that their daughter seemed a bit happier.

Once they had unpacked and settled in, Matty said a tearful goodbye to her parents. Sandy seemed to understand how she was feeling and offered to take her on a tour of the school and gardens.

'I didn't want to come here two years ago, when my mum died,' Sandy explained. ' Dad got a job abroad. My two big brothers were also sent to boarding school, but at least they had each other. I hated the first term, but since then I've got used to it and have loads of friends. Now I've

met you, Matty, I think you'll be my most special friend,'
she added.

Matty wanted to ask Sandy about her mother, but
didn't like to in case she upset her new friend. Maybe one
day she would find out more about Sandy's family.

The garden was wonderful! Matty loved being outside,
and this was such an interesting garden.

The girls ran around outside until they heard a bell
ring.

'Come on, that means supper time!' said Sandy, and she
led Matty back to the school. At supper Sandy introduced
her to the others who were Year 7 boarders and would
share the dorm. She was the only new girl in the year and
everyone wanted to know about her. She was a bit shy
about telling them who she was and why she had come to
boarding school. However, they all seemed very friendly.
Matty felt that maybe this school would not be so awful
after all.

The next day, the day girls arrived and term started.
There were a couple of new day girls in the class, so Matty
didn't feel that she stood out quite so much. These girls,
like her, had not learnt any French before, so they were to
have special classes in order to catch up. Apart from the
French, Matty felt she could keep up with the lessons. She
had always liked school and had tried hard to do well. Her
favourite subject was art. In the afternoon they went to the
studio and Matty was delighted to find a room dedicated to
art! They were told to draw and paint a watering can, and
her new teacher praised her for her work.

'You're so clever!' enthused Sandy. 'I wish I could draw
like that!'

'I'll teach you if you like,' answered Matty. 'It's not really that hard.' She so wanted to please her new friend.

'Well, I could help you with French, then,' replied Sandy. 'My dad works in France, so when we go there for the holidays we get to practise speaking in French.'

So the girls made a pact to help each other. Matty wanted to learn French, not just to catch up in her class, but also because she knew that many people spoke French in Burundi, where her parents were going.

The first few days were strange as Matty tried to find her way around the school. She learned that some of the buildings were hundreds of years old and had originally been part of an abbey. That was why the school was called St Anne's. It also explained the long corridors and the very lovely old chapel, where morning and Sunday prayers were held.

Sandy was in the school's junior choir and wanted Matty to join as well. Matty wasn't so sure. She liked singing, but the thought of singing alone in front of the music teacher to see whether she was good enough to join the choir was worrying her.

When the weather was fine, after classes had finished the two friends often went out into the garden. Matty tried to teach Sandy how to draw flowers and trees. Then Sandy helped Matty with her French homework. After that, they usually played hide-and-seek. Sometimes others from their dorm joined them: Mia, Rosie, Florence Jo and Polly. On the whole, they got on quite well together, although Mia was sometimes moody and miserable. She seemed to resent Matty being Sandy's best friend.

Matty found the weekends the hardest. On Saturdays, if they liked, the housemistresses would take the girls down to the beach, or even to the town to shop. They were all given £3 pocket money so that no one had more money than anyone else. Matty always phoned her mum and dad on Saturday, but they seemed very far away, and sometimes talking to them made her miss them even more. After speaking to them, she often went out into the garden, where it didn't matter if she cried. Sandy was a really good friend and would come and look for her and cheer her up.

On Sunday morning there was a chapel service. Although Matty and her parents did not usually go to church, almost all the girls went to the chapel service, so Matty went along too. Sandy was in the choir, but Matty sat with the others from her dorm. She liked the singing, but usually found herself daydreaming while the chaplain was talking. She imagined what her parents might be doing in Burundi. They had told her that there was a beautiful beach beside Lake Tanganyika, and that often they went to swim there. They probably spent Sunday playing tennis at the club and then swimming! How she longed to be with them! The Christmas holidays were such a long way off! Sometimes she felt very homesick and just longed for her parents to give her a cuddle. There were times when she woke at night from nightmares, imagining that something terrible had happened to them and that she would never see them again! Usually after one of those bad nights she would use her mobile and phone them.

Matty wasn't the only one who had bad nights. From time to time she would awake to hear Mia crying. She didn't have much sympathy for her, though, because her parents only lived in London and occasionally came to see her at the weekends. Sandy was always cheerful, even though her mum was dead and she would never see her again, and she only saw her dad in the holidays. Matty did wonder how her friend could be so happy, but there were lots of things about Sandy that puzzled her. Every night, just before 'lights out', Sandy would kneel by her bed and pray, and every morning she read a little bit from the Bible. No one else in the dorm did that. Sometimes the other girls would tease her and say she must belong to 'The God Squad', but Sandy always took it in good part and continued to be as cheerful as ever.

Very often on Sunday morning, after the chapel service, Sandy and Matty went to play in the garden. They both loved to play hide-and-seek there because there were so many good places where they could hide. Matty liked it best when it was just her and Sandy, but sometimes the rest of the dorm wanted to join in too. It was never as much fun when Mia was with them; she always ended up moaning about something and saying it wasn't fair.

There were always lovely flowers in the garden, and now that it was autumn, the leaves on the trees were turning red and gold. When it was warm enough, Matty took her sketchbook and pencils and drew. Miss Grace, the housemistress, had asked if she could put some of Matty's pictures on display in the corridors to brighten them up because she thought they were so good. Matty was pleased and proud. When she had first met Miss Grace, Matty had thought her rather old and not at all motherly, but over the weeks she had found that she was a very kind lady who was really rather like a nice great-aunt to all the girls. She always seemed to know when one of her girls was upset or homesick, and she often thought up treats to brighten up Saturday evenings.

Half-term was getting closer and Matty was dreading it. She would have to stay at school because it was too far for her to travel to see her parents. Everyone else from her dorm was going away. Even Polly, whose parents were in China, was going to visit her grandmother. Sandy was going with her brothers by train to Paris and then on to the small town where her father lived. Only a very few girls would be left in the whole school. Most of the staff were also going away. Matty was glad when Miss Grace told her that she would be the house mistress for everyone staying at the school.

'We'll just have to make our own fun!' she said to Matty, her eyes twinkling. 'We can have just as good a holiday as everyone else! You wait and see!'

Matty smiled and tried to believe her, but she was not sure that being at St Anne's without Sandy would be fun. When she watched Sandy packing her case ready to go to France, she tried not to be jealous or to show how miserable she felt inside.

'Have a lovely time,' she told her friend. 'And don't forget to draw me some pictures!'

'I won't,' replied Sandy. 'And I shall miss you, but make sure you have some fun and adventures to tell me about when I get back!'

3 Half-term

M iss Grace came bustling along the corridor as soon as Matty had waved Sandy goodbye.

'Now, Matty,' she said, 'I told you we would have some fun! Your parents have given permission for you to stay at the school's field centre. There are four other girls who can't go away to their families, so the six of us will have a holiday together! You'll need to pack a bag with jeans and jumpers, underwear and night-wear, your wash bag, a torch and some books to read. You'd better bring wellies as well as trainers. I guess you'll want your sketchbook and pencils too! I'll bring the bed linen and towels and food. Meet me in the refectory at six o'clock. We're going in the school minibus. I bet you didn't know I could drive it!'

Miss Grace was all smiles and looked very excited, and Matty realized that she wasn't quite as old as she had seemed!

Matty quickly packed the things she needed for the week and found she was soon humming a merry little song that they sometimes sang in chapel: 'God loves me, he really, really loves me.' The song went round and round in her head. For the first time she thought about the words. 'I wonder if there really is a God, and if he really does love me?' she said to herself. 'If there is, I want to say thank you to him for Miss Grace.'

At six o'clock Matty carried her case and her wellies down to the refectory. She saw the twins, Louise and Laura, who were in Year 9, sitting with their bags.

'Hi!' they said. 'Isn't this fun? No one but Miss Grace would plan such a great time for half-term. Sometimes we just have to hang around the school all week. We always have to stay here except for the long holidays, when we get to fly home.'

'Where is your home?' asked Matty.

'Sudan,' chorused the twins. 'It costs so much for our fares, especially as there are two of us, and we also have three brothers who are at school in Scotland,' explained Laura, 'so we can only go home once a year.'

'We're used to it now,' said Louise, 'but it was hard at first. Your parents are in Africa too, aren't they?'

'Yes, Mummy and Daddy are in Burundi for two years, but I'm going there at Christmas. I haven't been to Africa before. I need to start having lots of injections after half-term!'

'You will love it in Africa!' said Laura. 'We were born there. Our parents are missionaries. For a while we did school at home, then we went to a primary school in Kenya, but we had to come here for Year 7 like you.'

'I'm not quite sure what missionaries are,' said Matty. 'Can you explain sometime?'

'Of course!' the twins answered.

Just then, Miss Grace joined the girls, along with two other girls whom Matty didn't know very well. She knew that they were prefects and were in the sixth form.

'Matty, this is Rebecca, and this is Chloe,' said Miss Grace, and the two sixth-formers greeted her.

'We're all ready now—you all just need to put your belongings into the minibus and we can go!' Miss Grace beamed at them all.

Very soon, they were on their way speeding down to Dorset. Although it was late October, the days were still warm and most of the trees still had their leaves as the weather had been dry and mild. It was dark when they reached the site. There were eight log cabins arranged in a circle, one larger cabin which served as a sitting and dining area, and also a toilet block. The warden had a cabin heated and lit with a paraffin lantern. The twins were ecstatic: 'It's just like home, having a lantern instead of electric lights!' Because they were so thrilled, even Rebecca and Chloe didn't complain at having no electricity! The five girls were to sleep in the cabin and Miss Grace in a caravan which was reserved for staff. There were three bunk beds in the cabin, all equipped with sleeping bags. Rebecca and Chloe both wanted to be on lower bunks, so the twins chose to sleep above them, and Matty chose the top bed of the spare bunk. They quickly unpacked and were ready when they were called over to the main building to eat.

'Fish and chips tonight!' said Miss Grace. 'The wardens went out and collected our supper for us. Tomorrow we'll cook our own!'

Everyone was starving and supper was soon over. The girls did the washing up, which seemed great fun in the small kitchen next to the main room. Then they sat round a lovely log fire and sipped mugs of hot cocoa before the younger girls were sent to get ready for bed. They were already asleep when Chloe and Rebecca joined them.

The next day, they all woke early. At first, Matty couldn't think where she was. Then she remembered! It was just getting light, and she peeped out of the window at the camp site. It had been dark when they arrived the night before, so she had not really seen much.

As well as the cabins and other buildings, Matty could see there was a swimming pool. The site was surrounded by trees and she could hear some birds singing. The sky was clear and blue, promising a lovely day. She looked round her cabin and saw that the twins were also awake. Both were reading, using their torches. Laura saw her looking and whispered, 'Hi! We're being quiet for a few minutes.' She added rather shyly, 'We like to read our Bibles in the morning.'

Matty nodded, thinking of Sandy, because she started her day that way too. Matty wondered what was so interesting about the Bible. Her parents had one at home on the bookshelf, but she had never read it. Maybe she should some day. Then she remembered that it would be two years before she went back to her real home, so perhaps she had better look to see if there was a copy she could borrow from the school library.

Rebecca and Chloe were first over to the showers. They seemed to take ages! It didn't take the twins and Matty very long to get washed and dressed. There was a wonderful smell of bacon coming from the kitchen, and Miss Grace was singing merrily to herself as she wielded the frying pan.

'Sleep all right, girls?' she asked.

'Yes, thanks!' they chorused back.

'Mmm, that smells good!' said Chloe.

'Can you set the table, Chloe, and Rebecca, can you make some toast and the tea? Then we'll be ready to eat,' Miss Grace answered.

Matty could hardly believe that this was the same old lady who had met her when she arrived at St Anne's and led her through all the long corridors to her dorm. She hadn't seemed much fun then!

After breakfast, they all went on a walk to explore the area. Surrounding the site was a stream. It was crystal clear and very pretty. Then they walked up a steep hill, and suddenly they were able to see the sea. The path down to the shore was steep and rocky, but well worth the effort of climbing down. The girls were soon paddling, even though the water was freezing cold! They sat down on the pebbles to dry their feet and laughed and chatted together. Even Rebecca and Chloe didn't seem so much older as they joined in the fun.

Rebecca told them how she had chosen to stay at school during half-term to keep Chloe company. Chloe looked sad for a moment. 'I have no parents,' she explained. 'They were killed in a car crash when I was very small. My gran brought me up, but last month she died suddenly. Nothing is really sorted out about a home for me. I've got an uncle who's trying to sort things out. This is my last year at school before university. It's as if my whole world has changed. I chose to stay here for the holiday because I feel that school is a second home.'

The other girls were very quiet; they didn't know how to tell Chloe how sorry they were.

Miss Grace came to the rescue. 'We're so glad you feel that we're your friends—we're here to listen and help in any way we can.'

Laura was wiping away a tear. 'My dad would suggest that we pray and ask God to comfort you,' she said.

'That's a wonderful thing to do—I always find that praying helps me in every situation,' commented Miss Grace. 'Would you like us to pray for you?' she asked Chloe.

Chloe looked up and said yes. The others closed their eyes, so Matty did as well. Miss Grace said a simple prayer and Matty joined in with the 'Amen'.

From somewhere inside her rucksack Rebecca produced a large bar of chocolate and they all shared it. The sea air had made them hungry. Then Miss Grace explained to them that this was the Jurassic coastline and that they might find some fossils. They decided that it would be good to go fossil-hunting, and between them they found several small pebbles with fossilized shells and leaves. They took their finds back to their cabin.

After lunch, the sixth-formers wanted to be quiet in the cabin and do some work as they were preparing for exams. The twins and Matty were quite happy to go off exploring on their own. They put on their wellies and headed for the stream around the camp site, where they started searching for wildlife. After a while they sat on the bank for a rest.

'Miss Grace is fun, isn't she?' said Laura.

'Yes,' answered Matty. 'When I first met her, I thought she was quite an old lady. Now she seems almost young!

What I don't understand, though, is why she wears a
wedding ring but is called "Miss".'

'I don't know,' answered Louise. 'Now you mention it,
it does seem a bit odd. But she's always so kind, and often
gives up her holidays to be with those of us who can't go
home.'

'You were going to tell me about your home,' said
Matty, 'and what being a missionary is.'

'Oh yes,' replied Louise. 'We live in Sudan, the largest
country in Africa. It has had a civil war for many years,
and the people are very poor. Often they don't have
enough food to eat or any medical help. Around us, most
people live in mud huts and look after goats and cows.'

'Dad is a doctor,' added Laura, 'and Mum is a nurse.
They run a small clinic so that people can have medical
help. Mum also teaches a group, mostly women, to read
and write. Dad helps on Sunday with church services. It's
hot and dry and a desert most of the time. We all long for
the rainy season, when there's more water and it's cooler.
We don't have any electricity or water supply where we
live. There's a well in the village and when we're home we
help our house boy to get water. It's great, though. We run
around bare-foot and play outside with our brothers most
of the holidays.'

'But being a doctor and a nurse doesn't make our
parents missionaries,' explained Louise. 'A missionary
is a person who is a Christian and wants to share the
Christian faith with other people. You can be a missionary
anywhere—it just means telling others about who Jesus is
and what he has done for us.'

'I think I'm a Christian,' said Matty. 'I was christened as a baby. I've never been to church much, but I like going to chapel at school with Sandy. Isn't Christianity a bit like the Brownie motto of helping everyone all you can, especially those at home?'

The twins looked at each other, not sure who should answer.

'I'm not very good at explaining things,' said Laura, 'but being a Christian means that you choose to follow Jesus and live for him, and allow him to be your Friend and Saviour.'

'It doesn't just happen because you were baptized as a baby or dedicated—as we were—or because you attend church,' added Louise.

The girls heard Miss Grace calling them, so the discussion was abandoned, but it made Matty think. It seemed that there was more to Christianity than she had thought. She made a mental note to ask the twins more some other time, or maybe Sandy when they were all back at school.

4 Miss Grace's secret

The rest of the week seemed to fly by. There were so many interesting things to do. The girls enjoyed cooking, especially one evening when they had a camp fire outside and cooked sausages over it.

One night, there was great excitement. Everyone had gone to sleep as usual, but suddenly, in the middle of the night, the girls were all woken by a strange sound. It sounded like gunfire! Even the two older girls were rather scared. All five of them put jackets over their pyjamas and grabbed their torches before going outside to find Miss Grace. She, too, had been woken by the noise and she decided to phone the police on her mobile. They promised they would follow up the call at once and told everyone to stay together in Miss Grace's caravan. Miss Grace made them all a cup of hot chocolate and tried to keep them calm. The gunfire continued, but it did not sound too close. It was a relief to hear the police car entering the campsite. A very nice policewoman came to reassure them that they were in no danger. A gang had been found shooting deer illegally, to sell as venison. They had been arrested and taken into custody. Sadly, six deer had been killed and one injured stag had had to be taken to the vet's.

The policewoman thanked them all for alerting the authorities. The gang had shot deer before, but the police had not been able to catch them. Once the police had gone, all the girls felt reassured that there was no danger and went back to their cabin. They slept late the next morning and were just having breakfast when a ranger from the National Trust came to thank them all for phoning the police. He told them about the herds of wild deer on the moor and promised to take the girls out that evening to watch them.

So, at about six o'clock, two rangers arrived in Land Rovers to collect the girls and Miss Grace. The rangers knew exactly where the deer were and the girls were thrilled to see a whole herd! Watching the majestic animals as the sun set was a magical experience that none of them would ever forget. It was well worth being disturbed the night before.

The holiday was over and they were all in the minibus on their way back to school when the subject of missionaries was brought up again. Chloe had been asking the twins about their family. She was very interested to hear about life in Sudan. It seemed very exotic compared with her life living in the suburbs of London with her grandmother. Matty said that she hadn't understood what a missionary was before the twins had explained it to her. Miss Grace was driving but listening to the girls as they talked.

'I was a missionary once,' she told them.

'Were you?' asked Louise with surprise. 'Where did you work?'

'I was in Nepal,' answered Miss Grace. 'Look, it's time for a break, so, if you like, when we stop I'll tell you all about it.'

'Yes, please!' chorused the girls. They had all grown so fond of this woman who had sacrificed her own holiday to give them all a good time.

They sat round a table at the motorway service station and Miss Grace began her story.

'I trained as a doctor after I left school,' she began. The girls gasped. They had no idea that their house mistress was a doctor!

'Why are you called "Miss" and not "Dr", then?' asked Laura.

'All in good time!' laughed Miss Grace. 'Let me tell you what happened to me. After I qualified I felt that God wanted me to go and work abroad to help people who had few medical facilities and where I could share my faith in Jesus. In order to do that I needed to do some extra training in a Bible college. I had only become a Christian while I was at medical school, so I had much to learn about my faith and the Bible. I went to a college in Glasgow for two years. I really loved it at the college, and I also grew to love one of the other students there. At the end of our course we got married and went to Nepal as missionaries.'

'That explains the wedding ring,' thought Matty to herself.

'My name is really Dr Grace Thomas. My husband was an engineer called David. You might guess by his name that he was a Welshman!

'We loved our life in a remote part of Nepal, and we were kept very busy learning to speak the language and helping people, as well as sharing our faith when we were able. Then, to add to our joy, I found that I was pregnant, and, never one to do things by halves, I found I was expecting twins! All went well and we had a little girl we called Joy and a boy we called Joe. After four years we came back to the UK and spent a year in Wales. It was such fun taking the twins to meet our family and visiting the people who had supported us while we were abroad. When the year was finished we returned to Nepal and took up our work again.

'Then, about a year after that, some rebel soldiers woke us up one night. They demanded that "the doctor" go with them to treat some wounded soldiers. David was very worried and didn't want me to go, but I told him not to worry, and to stay and look after the twins.

'The soldiers took me far away into the jungle to their camp. On the way they blindfolded me so that I wouldn't be able to tell anyone the exact location of their hideout. I was scared and was quietly praying that the Lord would keep me safe.

'I treated the soldiers as best I could, operating with almost no equipment to remove some bullets and to clean infected wounds. Then I asked to be taken back home, but they laughed and said, "When we've finished with you, we'll take you back!"

'Inside, I felt cold and worried. I wondered how my family were. I was kept like a prisoner for several days, getting little to eat and having no water to wash with. They even sent a guard to accompany me when I went to the latrine, in case I might make a run for it! As if I could in the middle of the jungle! Eventually, when my soldier patients were definitely improving, they suddenly decided to release me. They didn't take me to my house, but dropped me off by the side of a road a few miles away. At least I knew where I was. Of course, in those days we had no mobiles, or any other sort of telephone, so I had no alternative but to begin to walk home. I was tired and hungry, but I prayed as I went, asking God to get me safely back home.

'When I finally reached the mission hospital I knew that something was very wrong. One of the guards on the gate looked at me as if I had come from Mars!

'"We never thought to see you again, Doctor Thomas!" he cried out in surprise. "We thought you'd gone, like the others."

'"What do you mean?" I asked. "What others?"

'"Oh, Doctor," he said, "I shouldn't be the one to tell you. Things here are so bad. The rebels took you and then attacked us. Come in and sit while I tell you."

'"No, first I must see my family. Then I'll come and listen," I replied.

'"No, no, no! You must not go there!" He was almost crying.

'Feeling totally numb, I followed him into the hospital and sat down. The head nurse came to me.

'"We cannot tell you how sorry we are—we grieve for you," he said. "The rebels looted your house after the soldiers took you away. They shot your husband and babies. We have buried them for you with a Christian service. We thought you must have been killed too!"

'You can imagine that I was so shocked, I couldn't take it in. David and the twins dead? I went into denial. They must be alive. This was all a bad dream.

'It took me a while to realize that it was indeed true. The local authorities came and wanted to take a statement. They made arrangements for some other missionaries to collect me and take me back to England.'

The girls didn't know what to say. They were so upset to hear this story.

Miss Grace looked at them and smiled. 'Don't look so distressed. It was all many years ago, and I've come to terms with the loss now and forgiven those who did such terrible things. At the time, I thought I would never forgive or ever recover from losing all those who were so dear to me. I was sick when I came back to England. The time in the jungle had given me a tropical disease that made me weak for some years, as well as being depressed. Some of my friends taunted me and told me to give up following the Lord Jesus because he hadn't looked after me very well. Yet I couldn't do that. He was the one who comforted me and helped me through those months and years of sickness and sadness. I knew in my spirit that it was the evil in men's hearts that had caused the tragedy, and eventually I chose to forgive them for what they had done. Then I began to get better.

'I never went back to Nepal. Indeed, I wasn't well enough to practise as a doctor and I was asked if I would be a housemistress here. I agreed on two conditions: one, that I wouldn't be called "Doctor"; and two, that I would be called Miss Grace, rather than by my married name. It somehow felt like a fresh start for me.'

'Thank you for telling us this,' said Chloe. 'Somehow, it helps me to know, and to not feel quite so sorry for myself, with my parents dead and now my grandmother. I know that for years I was angry with the driver who caused the accident that killed my parents, but my gran taught me to forgive him. She told me that my parents were Christians, so she knew they had gone to a better place. Even though I miss them, I know where they are, and now Gran has joined them. Since she died, I've been thinking about God a lot. If something happened to me, where would I go? I'm not sure I'd go to heaven.'

Even though it was time to get back in the minibus and continue their journey to school, Miss Grace felt that Chloe's question was so important that she had to try to explain very simply how to become a Christian and be sure of going to heaven when you die.

The girls listened as she told them. 'All humans mess things up from time to time,' she said. 'Which of us has never lied or thought something bad about another person, or lost her temper? We know we have, as the Bible puts it, 'sinned' against one another and also, more importantly, against God. As God is perfect, our sin cuts us off from him and brings us spiritual death. This means that, at the end of our lives, we can't be with him: we are condemned to eternal separation from him. That's why Jesus came to earth. He was the only perfect person, and when he died on the cross, it wasn't just because the Jews and the Romans hated him; it was so he could take our punishment of separation from God on our behalf. Because Jesus had never sinned, he was able to take the punishment for all our sin, so that we could be forgiven.

But our forgiveness isn't automatic. It's a gift that we need to receive from God.'

'How do you do that?' interrupted Rebecca.

'First,' explained Miss Grace, 'you need to realize that you have done wrong and say sorry to God for that. Then ask for his forgiveness and decide that from now on you will follow his ways. God always answers our prayers for forgiveness and he adopts us as his children. If you do this, it will be the beginning of a spiritual journey that will last all your life. Sometimes things are difficult, and sometimes they are fantastic; but whatever is going on in your life, if you are a Christian, you are never alone. Jesus, through his Spirit, will always be with you.

'There's so much more I could say, but we need to be on our way. If you're interested, on Thursday evenings, after homework time, we have a Christian Union group in my room for any girls who want to learn more about being a Christian.'

5 A new life

After half-term the dorm was very noisy! Everyone wanted to talk about the holidays! The other girls in Matty's dorm were quite envious when she told them where she had been and what she had done, and they looked at Miss Grace with a new respect when they heard how much fun she had given them. Matty didn't tell them about Miss Grace's secret; somehow it seemed too private a story to tell. She did, however, tell Sandy some of the things she and the twins had talked about, and that she was thinking about what it meant to be a Christian. She had decided to go to Miss Grace's little group each week and learn more. Sandy was keen to go with her, and they asked the other girls in their dorm to come too. Polly thought she might, but Rosie, Mia and Florence Jo were not interested. On the whole, the girls got on well together, but Mia still resented Matty for joining them and becoming Sandy's friend.

The weather became increasingly cold and wet, and playing outside was often not possible. However, with Christmas coming, there were lots of things to do. Rosie and Florence Jo were both in the school play, and Sandy was in the choir, which was rehearsing for the carol concert. Polly was very good at creating things, and she made pretty necklaces and bags for gifts. This gave Matty an idea. She could paint cards and pictures for her friends. Miss Grace was only too happy to take her into the town to buy some of the things she needed for this.

One Saturday she was painting in the common room, singing quietly to herself, when she noticed Mia sitting and doing nothing. She looked so miserable that Matty felt sorry for her. She decided to stop painting and see if Mia wanted to do something with her.

'Do you fancy doing something?' she asked Mia. 'We could play a game, do a jigsaw or watch a DVD if you like.'

Mia scowled at her. 'No thanks, not with you!' she snapped. Then she got up, deliberately spilled Matty's water jar over her painting and walked out of the room.

Matty was so upset. Her painting was completely ruined. It was of a squirrel, and she was doing it for Sandy for Christmas. It had taken a lot of time and effort. She swallowed her tears. Why did Mia hate her so much? She had only tried to be friendly. 'Well,' she decided, 'I won't bother being friendly any more!'

At this point, Miss Grace came in. She saw at once that Matty was upset, and then noticed the painting which had been spoilt.

'What happened?' she asked gently.

Matty knew she had a choice. She could tell tales and get Mia into trouble—but she had always hated tale tellers. She also remembered how Miss Grace had forgiven her husband's murderer. Spoiling a painting didn't seem such a terrible thing compared with that! So she took a deep breath. 'The water got knocked over and has spoilt my painting. I was just a bit upset because it was

coming on so nicely and I wanted to give it to Sandy for
Christmas.'

'I'm so sorry about that,' said Miss Grace. 'I was just
coming to tell you and anyone else from the dorm who
might be around that I'm toasting crumpets for tea.
Anyone who fancies one can come up to my room.'

'Oh thank you! That sounds scrummy!' answered Matty,
a smile creeping over her face. 'I'll go and see if anyone
else is around and would like to come.'

Matty ran up to the dorm. Sandy had just arrived back
after her carol practice, Mia was lounging on her bed
and Rosie was writing a letter. Matty gave them all Miss
Grace's message, trying to smile at Mia, even though she
still felt very angry with her.

All the girls went down to their housemistress's room.
The smell of toasted crumpets was fantastic. Even Mia
seemed pleased to have one!

Afterwards, Matty went back to the common room
to clear away her painting things. She looked sadly at
the spoilt painting before tearing it up and throwing it
away. Maybe she would start another tomorrow. She kept
wondering why Mia hated her so much. She decided that
perhaps she should ask God about it. Sandy had told her
that she could pray about anything and that God knew
everything, so why not ask him? She sat down and felt a
bit stupid, but asked God to help her to understand Mia
and even to like her. Somehow, deep inside herself, she
knew that God had listened to her.

It was now getting near the end of term and
everywhere in the school there was a buzz of excitement.
Matty managed to paint another picture of a squirrel for

Sandy and had even painted cards for all the other girls
in her dorm, as well as one for Miss Grace, the twins,
Rebecca and Chloe. She was looking forward to going out
to Africa to join her parents for Christmas, although she
was a bit scared about making the journey alone. Every
night she asked God to help her not to feel afraid, as well
as asking him to help her to like and understand Mia.

One day during assembly, Matty was delighted when
it was announced that she had been given a merit for her
hard work in the French class and was being promoted
to the top division! She knew it was because Sandy had
helped her so much, but she was very proud and excited
that she had earned points for her house. After assembly,
on the way to the biology lab, Sandy gave her a great
big hug. Then Matty noticed Mia looking at them with
anger, but also with tears in her eyes. Suddenly, Matty
understood. Mia was jealous of her friendship with Sandy!
Mia certainly didn't have any friends of her own, but was
often sulky and grumpy so that the other girls didn't want
to be around her. From that night onwards, Matty's prayer
changed and she asked God not only to help her to like
Mia, but also that they might become friends.

Every week Sandy, Matty and the twins, as well
as Chloe, Rebecca and several other girls, met for the
Christian Union meeting in Miss Grace's room. Matty
really looked forward to these meetings. They were
always interesting, with lots of singing and discussion.
Sometimes at the end, the girls would talk and pray about
their worries. Just before they broke up for Christmas,
Matty felt that she could tell the others about her fear
of travelling alone on the plane to Burundi. All the girls

prayed for her, and Miss Grace said that if Matty asked him to, Jesus would go with her. Matty asked Miss Grace if she could stay behind for a few minutes after the meeting and talk to her housemistress.

'Of course, dear,' Miss Grace answered. 'That's what being a housemistress is all about. I'm here for you whenever you need me.'

'I don't know how to say things,' said Matty, 'but I'm not sure that I'm a Christian. I thought I was because I was baptized as a baby, but I don't know Jesus in the way that the twins, Sandy and you do. I have been talking to God, and I know he listens to me. How can I really be a Christian?'

'Come and sit down, Matty. Let me explain a bit more,' said Miss Grace. 'Do you remember what I said when we were coming back from our half-term camp?' And once again Miss Grace explained to Matty how Jesus had come to live and then die for us, taking our punishment for all the wrong things we have ever thought, done or said. Because he took our punishment, God is able to forgive us and give us a new start, a new life as his child in his family. He becomes our heavenly Father, and Jesus our Brother and Best Friend.

'If you are really sorry for the wrong things in your life which meant that Jesus had to die, tell God and ask him to forgive you and make you his child,' Miss Grace told her.

Even though she felt shy and strange, Matty closed her eyes and did as Miss Grace had explained to her. When she had finished her prayer, she felt deep down inside that God had indeed forgiven her and she was now his daughter!

Miss Grace had tears in her eyes as she hugged her. 'Welcome to the Christian family!' she said. 'Today is a special day for you—it's your spiritual birthday!'

Matty smiled at her housemistress. 'Thank you!' she said, and went running up to the dorm to share her news with Sandy.

6 Christmas

It was two days before the end of term, and Matty was full of excitement because she would soon see her parents! She had so much to tell them about her life at school. When she thought about it, she wondered why she had been so angry at being sent to boarding school, because now she really loved it and had made lots of new friends, especially Sandy.

She was amazed because today, just a few days after she had told the girls in the Christian Union her fears about her journey to Africa and they had promised to pray for her, those prayers had just been answered! It made her twirl around with happiness when she thought how wonderful it was to be in God's family and have an all-powerful heavenly Father to take care of you!

The headmistress had just called Matty to her office. At first, Matty had been a bit scared, wondering if she had done something wrong and was to be punished. But then the head told her that her plane tickets and passport were all ready for her journey, and that she was to go on the same plane as the twins, Laura and Louise! The three of them had seats together and the air hostess was to look after them! They were all going from London to Nairobi on an overnight flight, and both sets of parents would be there to meet them in Nairobi and take them home to

Burundi and Sudan. The same arrangements had been made for their journey back to school after the holidays: they would all meet up again at the airport in Nairobi and travel together to London. The school nurse was to take them to the airport in London and would see the girls safely into the hands of the airline helpers. When she had heard all this, Matty felt all her fears dissolve; she could look forward to her trip with excitement now!

Matty raced up to the dorm to tell Sandy. Classes had finished and everyone was upstairs changing out of uniform for the evening. She was bubbling over with excitement and longing to see her mum and dad, and she told everyone how great they were. Then Matty caught sight of Mia's face and saw that she was trying not to cry. As Matty gave her a smile, Mia turned her face away and pretended to be busy.

Rosie, Florence Jo and Polly ran downstairs to watch TV and Sandy was going to choir, so now Mia and Matty were alone. Matty whispered a prayer in her heart to ask God to help her make friends with Mia.

'What's the matter, Mia?' she asked gently. 'I can see you're miserable. I know you don't like me much, but I really would like to be your friend.'

Mia began to cry. There weren't just a few tears: they poured down her cheeks like rivers.

Matty went over and sat by her on her bed and put her arms around her. She didn't know what to say, but stayed sitting there and let Mia cry. Eventually, through her tears, Mia began to talk.

'I hated you from the first time I saw you,' she said, 'because I could see that Sandy liked you and wanted to be

your friend. I have no friends, and I liked Sandy. Before
you came I thought that Sandy might become my special
friend. I've never had a friend, and nobody loves me or
wants me.' Mia started to cry again. 'I'm sorry I spoilt your
picture. I wanted to hurt you because you and Sandy are
such good friends. Yet you keep on smiling at me and you
didn't tell on me.'

'But what's upset you today?' asked Matty.

'I hate going home,' explained Mia. 'My mum left me
and my dad when I was only three—she went off with
another man. I haven't seen her since. I don't really
remember her much, only the smell of her clothes.
Sometimes I can remember that smell and it makes me
cry. My dad married again and my stepmother, Gloria,
doesn't want me around. That's why I was sent to
boarding school as soon as I was old enough. When I go
home, I'm always in the way and no one wants me there.
Now Gloria is expecting a baby of her own, and I know
when it comes they'll want me there even less. When I see
other girls happy, it makes me angry and bitter.'

'I'm so sorry, Mia,' said Matty. 'I had no idea your life
was so difficult. I did mean it when I said that I wanted
to be your friend. Yes, Sandy and I are great friends, but
that doesn't mean that you can't be our friend too.'

Mia nodded and gave Matty a little hug.

'Come on, wash your face and we'll go down to the
common room and play a game,' suggested Matty. 'Then
make sure you sit with Sandy and me at supper!'

Sandy was a little surprised when Mia came to sit by
her and Matty at supper, but she chatted away happily to
her. After supper, Matty asked Mia if she could tell Sandy

the things they had talked about earlier. Mia nodded, so Matty explained to Sandy about the situation Mia had to face at home. Sandy took Mia's hand and squeezed it. 'Of course we want to be your friends!' she said, smiling. 'We'll make a good trio!'

'Thank you so much,' said Mia. 'That will be the best Christmas present I could ever have!'

At last, it was the Christmas holidays. The twins were seasoned travellers, and Matty enjoyed going with them on her first adventure to Africa. They didn't sleep much on the overnight plane to Nairobi, but there were films to watch on the little TV screens in front of their seats, and the air hostesses kept coming to check that the girls were fine.

Matty's excitement knew no bounds when she got through immigration and saw her parents waiting for her in the arrivals hall. She thought she would never stop hugging her mum and dad! Then she found that Laura was tugging at her sleeve.

'Come and meet my parents,' she said. The twins led Matty over to say hello. Matty's parents smiled their approval. They had already met up with Dr and Mrs Lewisham and made friends. They all went over to a cafe and had a drink together before saying goodbye and 'Happy Christmas' to one another, and planning to meet up before the flight back to the UK in January.

The onward flight to Burundi was in a much smaller plane. Matty sat between her parents and just couldn't stop talking about everything that had happened since they had left her at St Anne's. Nobody would have thought she had been awake all night!

Once they had landed at Bujumbura Airport, Matty realized how hot it was outside and how tired she was! They got a taxi which seemed to hurtle through the busy, noisy city, and finally they arrived at the flat where her parents were living.

The days which followed were full of fun as her mum showed her around the city of Bujumbura. Sometimes they went to the shores of Lake Tanganyika, which was just like going to the seaside. The sand was silvery and very hot! They swam and had picnics, and sometimes shopped at the market. Matty loved the bright colours of the materials and the beautifully carved wooden animals which were for sale.

Matty was having a great time being back with her parents, but one thing was bothering her. She knew she should tell her mum and dad that she had become a Christian and that she would like to go to church at Christmas and celebrate the birthday of Jesus. She felt shy about telling them and wondered how they would react. However, both Sandy and Miss Grace had counselled her to share this news with them.

The opportunity came one supper time.

'What would you like to do on Christmas Day?' asked Dad. 'It will be very different from England. No white Christmas, roast turkey or crackers!'

'Actually,' Matty answered, 'I was going to ask you if we could go to church on Christmas Day to celebrate Jesus's birthday.' She took a deep breath and continued quickly: 'At school I became a Christian, a real one. It has made such a difference to me. I'm much happier on the inside now, and I've learnt to pray about things that worry me.'

43

Matty looked from one parent to the other, wondering what they would say. She loved them so much and wanted them to understand that she now loved God too.

A big grin spread over her dad's face.

'Well, that sounds wonderful! As you know, we're not very good at going to church, but we have been learning a lot of things from the Burundians here. Many of them have been refugees and own almost nothing, yet they are very happy because they have God in their lives. I have to tell you that it has made me think. Now my little girl has jumped ahead of me and found God! Maybe we shall have to learn from you!'

Mum was smiling too. 'I used to go to church when I was your age,' she said. 'And then somehow I just drifted away. It will be very good to go as a family this Christmas.'

Matty was very relieved. She had been worried that her parents might not approve, but they seemed pleased. Her dad went to find out which church would hold a service in English, or, failing that, in French, so that they would understand what was happening.

When Matty woke up at about six o'clock on Christmas Day, it was to hear the birds singing and to see the sun streaming in through the window. Hanging at the end of her bed was a stocking! She had not expected Christmas to be like it was back in England, so she was delighted with all the little presents packed into the stocking. Then she opened the parcel that Sandy had given her as they packed for the holidays. Carefully wrapped in tissue paper was a Bible. Matty was thrilled! How could Sandy have known that she wanted to have a Bible of her own to read?

She must have saved up for such a long time to get it for her! It had pictures and was written in English that was easy to understand. Straight away, Matty turned to the New Testament and found the story of the birth of Jesus. She was reading it when she heard her father whistling a carol and calling out to see if she was awake.

He came into her room and she showed him her present. He admired it with her and suggested that later in the day she should try to phone Sandy in France and wish her 'Happy Christmas'.

After breakfast of paw-paw, bananas and mangoes, they went into the living room to open their presents. Matty had bought her mum some of her favourite biscuits and her dad some chocolate. These were treats which could not be bought in Burundi. She had also made them cross-stitch bookmarks and hand-painted cards. They were both thrilled with her gifts. Then her dad handed her a box. When she unwrapped it, she found the most amazing box of paints that she had ever seen! There was also a box of pencils and two blocks of water-colour paper.

'Thank you sooooo much!' she squealed in delight.

'Well, we can't have our budding artist running out of materials, can we!' teased her dad.

'We do have something else to tell you,' added her mum. 'Not exactly a Christmas present, but we've saved the news until now. You have always been the apple of our eye, and always will be, but I'm expecting a baby! It's early days as yet—the baby is due at the end of May. In time you will have a little brother or sister!'

'Wow!' shouted Matty. 'That really is the most wonderful Christmas present! I used to long for a brother or a sister when I was smaller, but then gave up hoping! I'll try to be the best-ever sister when the baby is born!' Then Matty thought for a moment. 'Will you have the baby in Africa, Mum? Is it safe over here for that?'

'We haven't quite decided about that,' answered her mum. 'In fact, I was talking to your friends from Sudan as we waited for you to arrive, and they suggested that I have the baby in Nairobi, or I could return to England for a while.'

Then the family went to church together. The service was held in a large marquee that was completely full. There must have been several hundred people there, from many nationalities. The service was in English and translated into Kirundi, the local language.

There were carols which Matty knew, but it seemed strange to be singing 'In the Deep Mid-Winter' and carols like that in the heart of Africa and in the blazing sun! Several choirs got up and sang and also danced. Matty was entranced as they gracefully and enthusiastically moved to the music.

Afterwards, all the congregation were invited to stay for refreshments. There were bottles of locally made coke and orangeade, and sticky cakes. There may not have been mince pies or Christmas pudding, but the food was equally delicious and acceptable! They talked to others there, and Matty was able to try out her French with a family from Belgium who were working with the United Nations, while her parents made friends with an American family who were missionaries.

Later in the day, Matty phoned Sandy in France. She was so happy to hear her friend and thank her for her

Bible. Sandy had also been thrilled with the painting of the squirrel which Matty had done for her. 'Daddy has already hung it in my bedroom for me,' Sandy said. 'And he thinks it's brilliant. Even my brothers thought it was great, and that's real praise!'

The girls chatted for a while about all they had been doing during their holiday. Although they were both having a lovely time, they were missing each other! Afterwards, thinking about the squirrel picture reminded Matty of Mia and that she might not be having such a good holiday. She prayed quietly for her. She wished she had a phone number or an e-mail address so that she could contact her and wish her a happy Christmas, but Mia didn't have a mobile and Matty didn't know if she had a computer at home.

Once Christmas had passed, the rest of the holiday seemed to go very quickly. New Year's Eve was special because they had a barbecue on the beach with the American family whom they had met at church. They had a daughter, Sherry, who was two years older than Matty, and a son, Jason, who was eight. The children swam in the sea and sunbathed on the beach. It was so warm! Matty couldn't imagine what it would be like to get back to school and have to wear coats, scarves and gloves again! Sherry and her brother were home-schooled by their mum, but they missed the fun of having school friends and especially of being able to play lots of sport. They asked Matty lots of questions about her life at school, and she told them all about her first term, and even how she had become a Christian. Somehow, now that she had told her parents about this, it seemed easier to tell other people. In fact,

because she had met Sherry and her family at church,
it wasn't surprising to find out that Sherry was also a
Christian. They swapped e-mail addresses and promised to
keep in touch.

The grown-ups, too, were getting on well together,
which was nice for Matty's mum as she did not speak
French well and had struggled to make friends in Burundi.
The day ended with a moonlit walk along the beach to see
in the New Year. It was magical!

Before she packed to go back to school, Matty decided to
go to the craft market and buy her dorm friends a bracelet
each. She also bought a carved antelope for Sandy and
a giraffe for Mia, as well as a small carved box for Miss
Grace. She wrapped them all carefully and felt very happy
that she could take something special back for her friends.
It was hard to say goodbye to her parents, especially
her mum, who looked quite tired and needed to rest a
lot because of her pregnancy, but Matty was so looking
forward to seeing all her school friends again.

The twins were at the airport waiting for her, and once
they had waved goodbye to their families, they went into
the departure lounge to wait for the night flight back to
London.

7 The spring term

England at five o'clock on a January morning was very cold and the three girls shivered in spite of their warm coats! They were so glad to see Mrs Salter, one of the house mistresses of the upper school, waiting for them and holding their names on a placard. That made the girls feel very important, and they looked at one another and giggled!

Mrs Salter had brought her car to the airport and wanted to get out of London before the rush hour started, so the girls were soon on their way back to school. They all felt very sleepy after the night flight, and so were very quiet. Matty could hardly believe that the previous day she had been in Africa with her parents and now she was back in England. It seemed like a dream! Dear Miss Grace was waiting for her at school, and, after a warm drink, sent her to bed for a good sleep!

All the boarders began to arrive later that day, ready for the new term which would start the next day. Matty was pleased to see all her dorm-mates and catch up on the news of their holidays and tell them about hers. She was especially pleased to see Sandy and Mia, and the three of them had much to talk about. Things had been difficult for Mia and secretly she was pleased to be back at school. With Sandy and Matty as her friends, she felt that at least two people in the world cared about her! Matty told them that her mum was going to have a baby and that after all these years she would no longer be an only child.

Everyone quickly settled into the new term. It was cold, and Matty felt less like going outside to play after the heat of Africa. She found herself longing for the spring to come.

At the end of January it snowed, and after lessons most of the lower school—and some of the seniors too—had a great time playing in the snow. It was so very different from Burundi!

When she talked to her parents, they complained about the heat, while she told them how cold it was! She also received e-mails from her new American friend, Sherry. Matty was really pleased when she heard from Sherry that her parents sometimes went to church and also visited Sherry's family. Sherry told her about an adventure she and her brother had had one day when they went fishing on Lake Tanganyika with a Burundian friend. It had been a very hot day and the water had been calm. They had cast a net into the lake and were about to pull it up when their boat almost overturned. It was only a small dug-out canoe, so it tipped up easily. A hippo had decided to surface underneath the boat! It was quite a large beast, and it could have been very dangerous had they been tipped into the water. Sherry told Matty that they had been very scared, but their Burundian friend had shouted out to God to help them, and the hippo had dived down again and disappeared! She said that it was truly a miracle that none of them had been hurt, though they were shaken. They pulled up their net, saw they had caught some fish, and then headed for shore as quickly as they could. Back on the beach, they had stopped and said 'thank you' to God for hearing their prayer and keeping them from harm. They did have barbecued fish that night, but Sherry said that she had really lost her appetite!

Matty told this story to Mia and Sandy, and it really made Mia think. She had never prayed before and she wondered if God could help her. She really hated and resented her stepmother. She felt that her dad had no time for her and that maybe it would have been different if Gloria hadn't come on the scene. She wondered if God really did love everyone. Did he love her? Did he love her stepmother? Did he see how miserable her life was? Could she be happy like Sandy and Matty? These questions began to go round and round in her mind. Mia decided to go along with her friends to the Christian Union meeting in Miss Grace's room and see if she could learn more about God. Sandy and Matty were so pleased when Mia decided this, because they had been praying for their new friend to understand how much God loved her. They realized how rejected and unhappy she felt.

January slid into February, and it was still too cold and miserable to play much outside. Matty really missed being out in the garden. Sometimes she got bored with watching DVDs or playing board games in the common room. Spring half-term was getting nearer, and she was not looking forward to being left behind again when all her friends went home. Although Miss Grace had made it wonderful for her last term, she knew that would not happen every holiday. She kept telling herself that it was only one week, and she could read and paint as much as she wanted. In fact, Matty was planning to paint a picture for her new baby brother or sister. She thought it would be nice to paint something African like a baby elephant. Already she was trying out sketches to plan a picture.

One evening at supper time, Chloe came over to her. Matty felt a bit shy to have a sixth-former single her out.

'Will you be here for the holiday?' Chloe asked her.

'Yes,' replied Matty. 'But I don't think it will be as much fun as last time. No deer being shot in the middle of the night!'

'Well,' said Chloe, 'I've got a project to do for my exams. I thought you could help—if you want to, that is. The twins will be here too, and Rebecca might stay as well and join in.'

'What's it about?' asked Matty, interested and also flattered that Chloe had asked for her help.

'I'm trying to find out the history of the school buildings. Not much is known about what this place was like when it was an abbey. I thought that we could explore the buildings and maybe the grounds. Your skills in drawing and painting could really help. My idea is eventually to make a little book for the school library.'

'I'd love to help!' said Matty enthusiastically. 'I wasn't looking forward to half-term, but now I feel better about it already!'

'That's settled, then! I'm not sure which house mistress will be looking after us, but I'm sure nobody will mind our project.'

Sandy and Mia were waiting for Matty and wanted to know what Chloe had talked to her about. Matty was only too eager to tell them. Mia looked wistful. 'I wonder if I could stay here for half-term too. It would be much nicer than going home!' she said.

'Why don't you ask your dad?' suggested Sandy. 'It's only for a week, not a long holiday.'

Mia did phone her dad, and he seemed quite happy for her to stay at school for the half-term. The headmistress was agreeable as well, so it was all arranged. Matty was pleased. She knew it would be fun with the twins and was looking forward to helping Chloe with her project.

Half-term arrived, and Matty and Mia were very cheerful when they waved goodbye to their dorm-mates. Rebecca was staying at school to keep Chloe company, so there were six of them to tackle the project. The house mistress was pleased that the girls were all happy and had something to do, and the sixth-formers were made responsible for the younger girls when they went out.

Their first port of call was the town library. The librarian was very helpful and took them to the reference section where the town archives were kept. Matty was amazed to find out how old the abbey really was. It had been founded by some Benedictine monks in the thirteenth century, although most of the buildings dating back to that time had long since disappeared. It had never been a very large abbey, but the monks had kept a garden, growing herbs which they used for medicine and also maintaining bee hives to make honey. Mia and Matty decided to explore the large garden at school to see if they could find any traces of the old abbey garden. The librarian allowed Matty to make a copy of the plan of the old garden.

While she was doing this, the twins were finding out about the life of the monks and nuns at that time. First there were monks in the abbey, and then it became a convent for nuns. The librarian said that the library

contained an example of the writing they had done. She
was very kind and said that all six girls could see the
manuscript, though they must not touch it. She led them
into a small room where, under lock and key in a glass
case, they saw the manuscript. The librarian put on some
special white gloves, unlocked the case and turned the
pages for the girls to see. Matty was awestruck. Not only
was it very old and beautifully written, with the capitals
illustrated in coloured inks, but also Matty thought how
amazing it was that the monks and nuns had written
out the Bible so that other people could read it and learn
about Jesus. For her, it was the highlight of the visit.

Rebecca and Chloe had been finding out about the
history of the abbey. Although it had only been a small
abbey, it seemed it had flourished and been a place of
healing and learning as well as worship until the time
of King Henry VIII, when many abbeys were destroyed
as the Reformation took place. In those times, not only
was the celebration of the Mass forbidden, but also many
beautiful things were vandalized and destroyed, including
lots of things at St Anne's. Eventually, the buildings
which were still standing were sold as a manor house to
a nobleman, and they continued as that for many years.
There were lists of things which the nobleman had bought,
but a note said that the silver chalice and a special
plate called a paten, which had been used to celebrate
communion, had mysteriously disappeared and never been
found. They were very old and dated back to the time of
the foundation of the abbey.

There was a period of around one hundred years when
little was recorded about the manor house, but then,

during the Second World War, it was used to accommodate Allied troops. It was in a key position near the coast and had played a part in the evacuation of British troops from Dunkirk.

Armed with all this information, the girls went back to the school, looking at it with fresh eyes. Together they walked around the buildings, identifying what was old and what was new.

The next day was wet and cold. Laura and Louise decided that they would use the Internet to search for information on Benedictine monks, nuns, convents and abbeys, to find out what sort of life the inmates led from day to day. Rebecca and Chloe were busy writing up all that they had found out. Matty had hoped to explore the garden with Mia and make a map of it to compare with the map she had copied in the library, but she had to change her plans because of the weather. Mia had a good idea: 'Why don't we get permission to explore the house and play hide-and-seek?' she said. 'I know it's your favourite game!'

'That's a great idea!' answered Matty, so they went to ask permission from the house mistress responsible for them.

'I don't see why not,' the house mistress said. 'But don't go into the dorms or classrooms. Some doors are locked anyway, but otherwise you can have the run of the place.'

As the buildings were spread over a large area, the girls decided to confine themselves to one area at a time, or they would never find each other. They spent a long time finding good hiding places in the stables and storerooms. The time went by so quickly they were astonished when they heard the bell for lunch. After lunch, the twins joined them and they all played in the part of the old house where the monks and later the nuns had their dormitories. It was much harder finding three people than just one!

They had been playing for a little while. It was Matty's turn to be the seeker and she had been searching for ages; she had now found the twins, but not Mia. She was about to give up when she noticed an old door on the top floor. The door creaked when she opened it, which made here feel a bit scared. It was pretty dark but she felt around with her hand and found a light switch. She saw a small flight of stairs which led up to the attic. A spider ran out in front of her and Matty screamed. She wasn't especially frightened of spiders, but it had surprised her.

'Are you OK?' she heard Mia ask, giving herself away in her concern for Matty.

'Oh yes, thanks, I'm fine—it was just a huge spider that frightened me for a moment,' Matty replied.

Mia appeared from behind an old trunk. 'This is such an amazing place!' she said. 'They must have all the costumes here from every play the school has ever produced!'

Matty looked around and saw rails of costumes, covered over with dust sheets. There were trunks, boxes and lots of dust everywhere.

'We'd better go and find Laura and Louise,' said Matty. 'They'll wonder where we've gone—but you found a great hiding place!'

As they made their way to the door, Mia tripped and fell against the wall. The plaster was loose and came away.

'Oh dear, I'll be covered in white dust,' Mia moaned. As she brushed the dust off Mia, Matty noticed that underneath the plaster, on the wall, there were colours. It looked like there had been an old painting there.

'Look!' she exclaimed to Mia. 'Look, there's something underneath the plaster! Let's get the others and see what they think!'

The girls ran down the stairs and found the twins a bit fed up with waiting for them.

'You found her at last!' said Laura.

'I'm sorry,' said Matty, 'but Mia was in the attic and we've found something really exciting up there! Come and see! We think it may be an old wall painting.'

All four girls went back to the attic, and the twins peeled off a little more plaster with their fingers. They were sure they had found something left from the old abbey.

Within a few minutes they had found Rebecca and Chloe as well and dragged them upstairs to see their find. The two older girls were impressed, so all of them went to tell the house mistress.

'Can we invite the librarian to come and look, to see if it's significant?' asked Chloe, who was really very excited about the find.

'I think that would be a good idea,' replied the teacher. 'I'll phone the library for you now.'

By the end of the day, there were several excited people examining the wall where the plaster had come away. It was arranged that an expert would come as soon as possible and, with the head's permission, would investigate further.

Later in the week, the weather cleared up and so Matty was able to go out and map the garden. She found that very interesting. After a while, she located the place where the herb garden had been and went to find the gardener to talk to him about it. He suggested that the girls might like to help him restore it. That seemed a good project for the summer term. There certainly was no time to do it this half-term.

On the last evening, the six girls were together in the senior common room. Chloe had invited the younger ones there to show them how much she had been able to do and to thank them for their help.

'No, we should thank you,' said Louise. 'It's been really interesting helping you!'

'Yes,' said Mia shyly, 'it's been the best half-term I've ever had!'

'How about you, Matty?' asked Rebecca. 'Have you enjoyed it?'

'Oh yes!' said Matty. 'There have been so many good things, and we even have a project of our own—to restore the monks' herb garden—but the best thing was seeing the manuscript and realizing that if the monks had not written down the Gospels, we might not have the Bible! That really made me think and be thankful,' she added.

Chloe smiled at Matty. She, too, had been going to the meeting in Miss Grace's room since the previous half-term and had asked Jesus to be her Lord and Saviour. Rebecca pulled a face and made a comment about Chloe joining 'The God Squad'. She could see that it had made a great difference to her friend, but she wasn't yet ready to become a Christian herself.

8 Worrying news

Everyone was glad when the weather turned warmer and spring at last seemed to be on its way. The garden was full of daffodils and the girls could be outside much more.

After half-term some archaeologists had arrived at the school and verified that the wall painting was from the fourteenth century. They had been working slowly and carefully to restore it. It was a picture of Mary with the baby Jesus. The headmistress had told the whole school about the find and promised that when the restoration was complete, everyone could see it.

Chloe had continued with her project, and as she found out more history she made a point of sharing it with the other five girls. All of them were looking forward to the book which she hoped to produce. She had promised that their names would be mentioned as they had helped her!

Sandy had been to France for her holiday and seemed very quiet and not quite herself. She was still helping Matty with her French and they were revising one afternoon in the garden when Sandy gave a big sigh.

'What's the matter, Sandy?' asked Matty. 'Something has seemed to be wrong since you came back from half-term. Was everything all right at home? I haven't done anything to upset you, have I?'

'Oh no, of course not,' answered Sandy. 'But you are right—I am a bit worried about something. It's sort of a secret, though. If I tell you, please don't say anything to anyone, not even Mia. It would be nice to be able to share it with you, though.'

'I promise I won't say anything to anyone, but I'll be glad to know what's worrying you,' said Matty. 'I hate seeing you so quiet and sad.'

'It's my dad,' said Sandy. 'Nothing's wrong with him, but he has a girlfriend. I know I should be glad, but I can't bear the thought of anyone taking Mum's place. I don't really want another mum.'

'What's she like?' asked Matty.

'She's quite small and young, and very friendly,' said Sandy. 'She's a Christian, too, so I should be pleased. I've tried to like her and be friendly, but it's so hard. I was always "Dad's girl", and now I'm not any more. He didn't have much time just to be with me and talk to me during half-term. My brothers don't seem to mind. They like her. Her name is Sophie. I know I'm being very selfish, but I just don't want Dad to marry again.'

Matty didn't know what to say. She just sat holding Sandy's hand. Eventually she found her voice. 'Well, thank you for telling me. You taught me to pray about my troubles, and we can talk to God about Sophie. Maybe God can help you to like her.'

The two girls held hands and each said a simple prayer that God would indeed help Sandy to like Sophie and be happy if her dad did want to get married again.

The rest of the term seemed to pass very quickly. They had a series of class assessments, and Matty was pleased that none of them seemed too hard, not even the French one. She was very pleased with her art assessment. The task was to paint a seascape which included seagulls. She found that fun to do, but was also very happy because Sandy produced a good painting too. Her coaching had made a difference!

Matty was getting excited about flying back to Burundi for the Easter holiday. The flights had been arranged as before so that she would travel with Louise and Laura to Nairobi, where her dad would meet her. As her mum was in the last few months of her pregnancy, she would not be flying over to Kenya. Every week as Matty talked on her mobile to her parents she found that she was getting even more excited about the holiday and also the new baby. Also, while she was in Burundi she would have her twelfth birthday. It would be great to celebrate that with her mum and dad!

About a week before the end of term the headmistress asked to see her. As soon as Matty entered the office, she knew that something was wrong. Her headmistress looked very grave.

'Come and sit down, Matty,' she said. 'I'm afraid I have some rather sad news for you. Your dad has just phoned from Nairobi. Your mum is having trouble with her pregnancy and has had to be rushed to hospital there. They're trying to save the baby's life, but your mum is very poorly. Your dad will phone you this evening, but he has warned me that you will probably have to stay here for the Easter holiday. I'm so sorry, dear. It is such a disappointment for you, and such a worry, too.'

Tears began to well up in Matty's eyes. Her mum was ill and she wasn't able to be near her! And maybe her baby brother or sister would not live! She would not now be able to go to Burundi for Easter or her birthday.

'It's all right to cry, Matty, I do understand,' the headmistress said, trying to comfort her. 'You don't need to go back into class unless you want to. Miss Grace will let you sit with her in her room.'

By now, Matty was really crying. She tried to say that she would like to go and be with Miss Grace. The headmistress seemed to get the message and phoned for the housemistress to come and collect Matty and look after her.

In Miss Grace's room, Matty began to quieten down. Miss Grace had made her a cup of hot chocolate and was sitting with her on the settee.

'Tell me what's happened,' she said to Matty. Gradually, between her sobs, Matty blurted out the whole story of her mum's condition and the so-longed-for baby brother or sister. Miss Grace listened to her story, handing Matty tissues as they were needed.

Miss Grace didn't speak for a long time, but then she said, 'Shall we talk to Jesus about this whole problem?'

Matty nodded. After Miss Grace had prayed for all the family, Matty felt calmer and she somehow knew deep inside that God would help them all.

By the time the bell had rung for lunch, Matty felt that she could join her class again. She knew that Sandy and Mia would wonder what had happened and would be worried.

'If you're sure you're ready to join them,' Miss Grace had said. 'But remember, if you get upset again, you can come back here.'

Sandy and Mia—and even Rosie, Florence Jo and Polly—could see that something was very wrong when Matty rejoined them. Matty decided to tell them all the problem when they were together at the lunch table.

'My mum's pregnancy has gone wrong and they've taken her to Kenya to see if they can save the baby's life,' she said. 'She's very sick.' By now the tears were starting to come again, but Matty was determined to keep going. 'Daddy's going to phone me with news tonight. He says I must be prepared to stay here for the Easter holidays. But I was so looking forward to going home and having my birthday with Mummy and Daddy,' she added.

The girls were shocked. 'We're so very sorry, Matty, we wish we could help,' they said.

Sandy stayed very close to her friend through the rest of the day. Fortunately, at the end of term the classes were more relaxed and Matty didn't have to concentrate too hard. Sandy was wondering what she could do to help Matty. Then she had an idea and went to talk to Miss Grace about it before tea. 'Please can I make an extra phone call to my dad?' she asked. 'I just wondered if Matty could come home with me for the holiday as she can't be with her mum and dad.'

A lot of phone calls were made and received that evening! Sandy talked to her dad and he was very willing for Matty to spend the Easter holiday with them in France. Then Sandy and Matty spoke to the headmistress, who talked to Matty's dad and asked if he minded her going to France. She reassured him that Sandy's father was very kind and responsible, and that she would make all the necessary travel arrangements, including cancelling the Burundi tickets. Then Matty's dad phoned Matty and they had a long talk. Matty learned that her mum was seriously ill with high blood pressure as well as malaria. She was receiving the best possible care in the hospital, but the doctors were uncertain whether or not to do a caesarean and deliver the baby early. Matty's dad promised to phone every day and let Matty know the news. Then he told her that the twins' father, Dr Lewisham, was coming to Nairobi for a few days before Laura and Louise were due to arrive, and he had promised to help them understand what was happening and make the right decisions.

At the end of the phone call Matty's dad said, 'I don't want you to be worrying all the time, Matty. Since Christmas your mother and I have started to pray, and we believe that God loves us and hears us. We learnt that from you, and Dr Lewisham has helped us to learn more. We know that Mummy and the baby are safe in God's hands, whatever might happen in the next few days. Mummy sends lots of love, and so do I. We both love you so much!'

At the end of the phone call, although the tears were coming again, Matty did feel comforted. She went to find Laura and Louise in their dorm and explained to them what was happening. She told them about their dad helping her parents, and she thanked them.

'We will all keep praying for your mum and dad,' said Laura. 'We know that God can heal your mum and look after the baby.'

That night, in spite of all the sadness and worry of the day, Matty fell asleep almost as soon as her head touched the pillow. She was so glad that she now belonged in the Christian family, and she felt comforted because she knew that her friends loved her and cared about her and her parents.

9 France

The last week of term seemed to pass very slowly for Matty. Each evening her dad phoned her, but there was no real news. Her mum remained very sick, but the baby was still alive. Matty tried to pray about it and not worry, but she found herself thinking about them all the time, and the thought 'What if they should die?' kept creeping into her mind. Then she thought about Sandy. Her mum had died. Matty had been learning that sometimes answers to prayers can be 'no' as well as 'yes', and sometimes even 'wait'. She kept begging God to let her mum live. Along with this, she was disappointed at not going to Burundi and being with her family for her birthday, yet also excited at going to France with Sandy.

Altogether, she felt very mixed up. She was also upset because every night Mia had been crying in bed, and sometimes even wetting the bed, because she was so dreading going home for the holiday. Matty and Sandy tried to comfort Mia and encourage her, but it didn't seem to work. It was hard for Mia to learn that Matty was going to France with Sandy.

On the first day of the holiday, Sandy and Matty packed their cases and went by train to London, along with several other boarders and a couple of teachers. They were taken to St Pancras station, where Sandy's two older brothers, Jack and Philip, were waiting for them. Jack was seventeen and Philip fourteen. They were both used to travelling abroad, and they soon found their seats on the high-speed train to Paris. Matty had never been through the Channel Tunnel before and was bubbling with excitement. The boys were amused, but they had been told why Matty was spending the holiday with them, so had promised not to tease the girls. In Paris, Mr Thompson, Sandy's father, was waiting for them all. Sandy jumped into her dad's arms, and Matty could see that they were especially close. No wonder Sandy was worried about him getting married again! When he greeted Matty, his eyes were kind and he seemed genuinely pleased to meet his daughter's best friend and have her stay with them for the holiday.

At Paris, after a quick drink and snack, they all boarded another train to Nancy, a town further east. Sandy's father had left his car at the station because the family lived just outside the town in an old farmhouse, near the Moselle river. It had been a long journey. It seemed to Matty that it had taken almost as long as going to Burundi! Yet even though she was tired, she was excited to be visiting a new place.

The farmhouse was a lovely place to live. It was so unlike most houses in England. It was stone-built and rambling. There were several outhouses, some in a state of disrepair, but it looked as if it would be fun to explore them and also play hide-and-seek! Matty was glad, too, that she had brought with her the new paints her parents had given her for Christmas. She could see there were many things to draw and paint.

It was evening when they arrived and it was lovely to be welcomed by a log fire in the living room. Soon supper was ready for them all. They had soup and wonderful fresh French bread with lots of butter and cheese. Sophie had come to greet the children and welcome them to the house, and had prepared the meal for them. Matty was intrigued to meet her. She and Sandy had prayed each day about the situation. Sophie was small and slim, with long dark hair tied back with a ribbon. She had a lovely smile and laughed a lot. Somehow she didn't seem old enough to be a 'mum' to these big children, but Matty couldn't help but like her.

After supper, Sandy showed Matty around the farmhouse. Matty was going to share Sandy's bedroom, so she wouldn't feel too lonely. She was glad about that.

The two girls were tired and glad to go to bed early. Before they put the light out, they read together from the Bible. They read from chapter twelve of the book of Isaiah.

Matty read about not being afraid, but trusting God. As they prayed together, she asked God to help her to trust him so that she would not be afraid. At that moment, her mobile rang; her dad was calling her.

'You have a tiny baby sister!' he announced excitedly. 'We're going to call her Neema, which means "Grace". She only weighs four-and-a-half pounds and is in the special-care baby unit.'

'Is Mummy all right?' asked Matty anxiously.

'She's asleep just now but very weak. The malaria is improving but her blood pressure is still high. She needs to be kept very quiet and is in a cool, dark room. The doctors are pleased that the operation to deliver Neema went so well, but we're not out of the woods yet.' Her dad's voice sounded tired and worried.

'Will Neema be all right, even though she's so small?' asked Matty.

'Again, we hope so, but no one can be sure,' answered her dad.

'Daddy,' said Matty, 'Sandy and I have just read from the Bible—from Isaiah chapter 12—and it tells us to trust in God and not be afraid. I was just talking to God and asking him to help me not to be afraid. You mustn't be afraid either.'

'Precious girl, you are helping us as we begin to know more about God! I'll read that chapter before I go to bed. Dr Lewisham is staying with me and will have to be at the airport very early tomorrow morning to meet the twins off the plane.'

'Please give them my love and tell them about Mummy and Neema. We'll pray for them,' added Matty, just before her dad rang off.

Sandy was wide awake now, so the two girls ran downstairs to tell everyone else the news.

'Oh là là!' exclaimed Sophie. 'You are now a big sister, Matty!'

'It's splendid news!' said Mr Thompson. 'But we need to pray that your mother will quickly be out of danger, and that the little one will thrive!'

He looked at Philip. 'You'd never think it, but you too were premature—and only four-and-a-half pounds when you were born! But look at you now! What a great strapping fellow you've become!'

Philip blushed, then laughed. 'Well, God must have wanted me to live for some reason!'

'He certainly did,' replied his dad. 'Now let's all kneel down and ask God to do miracles again!'

On the farmhouse kitchen floor, they all knelt down, and Sandy's dad prayed for each person in Matty's family. A great sense of peace stole into Matty's heart. Somehow she felt sure that both her mum and Neema would be well.

The first few days of the holiday were fine and Sandy took great delight in showing Matty around the little village where they lived. Her father had to work that week until Good Friday, so the two girls helped to make the meals. The boys went fishing and hiking when they were not doing revision for their exams. Matty was a little shy of the boys, having been an only child for so many years. They tended to tease their little sister quite a lot, and as the week went on this included Matty too. One afternoon they played hide-and-seek with the girls for hours. They all found wonderful places in which to hide. For a long time, no one could find Jack. He had climbed to the top of a willow tree. The foliage was just coming out and he was well hidden. In the end, Philip guessed where he might be.

Each evening, Matty's dad phoned with news. It was wonderful to learn that her mum was getting better, but baby Neema's condition was still causing concern. Her dad had taken some digital photos and e-mailed them to Mr Thompson, so Matty was able to see her tiny baby sister. Sandy's family continued to pray with her before the girls went to bed each night.

Most evenings, Sophie came to visit. It was clear to the children that she and Mr Thompson were very good friends. Sophie was also trying to make friends with the children, especially Sandy. She called Sandy by her first name, Beatrice. It sounded lovely when spoken in her soft French accent.

'I would rather call you Beatrice,' she explained, 'because I know that Sandy was your mother's pet name for you. And Beatrice is a name I really love,' she added.

Sandy smiled. She was finding it easier to like Sophie, who was becoming like a big sister to her.

'I want to go shopping in Strasbourg,' Sophie announced on Maundy Thursday. 'Would you girls like to come? I thought we could buy a nice present for the new baby, and your dad thought that maybe you needed some new clothes for the summer term, Beatrice. We can have a girls' day out. What do you think?'

Matty and Sandy looked at each other and beamed. It sounded as if it might be fun.

'Oui, merci,' they answered. 'That would be wonderful!'

'Be ready in half an hour and we'll catch the fast train. The boys can make their own supper and we will eat out,' Sophie told them.

The girls needed no second bidding, but ran upstairs to get anoraks and put on their boots.

The day was a huge success. Matty was getting used to hearing the French language and so enjoyed practising a little with Sophie and also in the shops. There was one shop which sold baby clothes, and had some very small items for pre-term babies. Matty chose a pink dress trimmed with tiny roses for Neema. It used up almost all her pocket money, but she really wanted to get it. Both Sophie and Sandy bought presents for the baby too, and

Matty was really touched to think that they cared for her little sister.

They seemed to have collected all sorts of bags and packages before they went to a cafe to eat. They were so tired on the way home that both the girls dozed off. Sandy's dad was at the station to meet them and take them back to the farmhouse. It had been such a good day.

The Easter weekend was very special for Matty. Each day she heard that her mum was getting stronger and Neema was stable, so her concern decreased. She kept saying 'thank you' to God for hearing her prayers. The family went to an International Church on Good Friday and Easter Day. This was the first year that Matty understood what Easter really meant and how much Jesus loved her. They also went into Nancy and saw a beautiful Easter procession that told the story of Jesus's crucifixion and resurrection. Matty knew she would never forget it. There were Easter eggs, too, just like she had at home with her family. Even Jack was not too old to enjoy his chocolate egg! Sandy's dad had a long weekend off from work, so on Easter Monday they all went for a picnic and a long trek through the countryside. They were fortunate that the weather stayed dry, even though it was rather cold. Mr Thompson lit a fire and cooked sausages for lunch, which were a bit burnt, but tasted wonderful! Afterwards, they sat around the fire and sang songs the boys had learnt at Scout camp. Even Sophie was learning them and joining in with her French accent. Then the songs changed as the children began to choose hymns. All the Thompson family sang well, and Matty could understand why Sandy loved being in the school choir.

The rest of the week seemed to fly by! On the Friday it was Matty's birthday. She hadn't mentioned it and had been preparing herself for it to be an ordinary day, so she was very surprised when she came down to breakfast to see balloons in the kitchen and the family waiting to sing 'Happy Birthday' to her! By her plate there were some parcels and cards to open.

'Thank you so much!' said Matty excitedly. 'I didn't know you knew it was my birthday!'

'We couldn't let such an important date pass by without a celebration!' said Sandy's dad.

'We've got a party planned for this evening!' Philip added.

Matty opened her presents. The Thompson family had made up a parcel containing twelve items, one for each year of her life! The presents were so thoughtful, they almost made Matty cry. There was a little silver photo frame for a photo of Neema; a wooden pendant made by Jack, who loved woodwork; a pencil case embroidered by Sandy; a CD from Philip containing some of the songs and hymns she had learnt during the holiday; and lots of other small items which would be useful at school. The last parcel which was waiting to be opened was very small, and when she looked at the label, she saw that it was from her parents. 'From Mummy and Daddy!' she exclaimed. 'With all the problems they're facing, they still managed to get a present to me here!'

'Of course they did!' replied Mr Thompson. 'It came by special delivery to await this special day!'

Matty opened it to find a lovely golden cross and chain. She gasped with delight. It was a very beautiful present and she would always treasure it.

By now, breakfast was almost over and Mr Thompson announced that he would be back at lunch time as he had taken a half-day off work.

'I would like you all to help with preparations for the party—all, that is, except Matty. Sophie has something else arranged for you, young lady! However, this morning, please can you all do your packing so that you're ready to leave for London tomorrow morning.'

'OK, Dad!' chorused the boys and Sandy, and Matty nodded in agreement.

Almost as soon as Mr Thompson's car had driven down the drive, they heard another car arrive. It was Sophie. She looked excited as she wished Matty a happy twelfth birthday. In her hand she held an envelope and gave it to Matty.

'This is my present to you,' she said. 'You are now very much a young lady!'

'Not too old to play hide-and-seek, though!' Philip said quickly.

Matty opened the envelope and found inside a pretty card containing a voucher. It was written in French and she was not quite sure what it meant. She looked slightly puzzled, so Sophie explained.

'It's for you to have your hair done ready for the party! I will take you to my hairdresser's this afternoon while the others prepare for the celebration.'

'Oh thank you, Sophie!' said Matty. 'That will be a really special treat!'

'Now I must go, but I will come back at half-past one to take you, Matty.'

'I'll be ready—and thank you so much!' answered Matty.

It didn't take Matty long to pack her case, and then she decided to go outside and draw the farmhouse as best she could. She wanted to remember this holiday. It had all started so badly, but in fact had been a very happy time with Sandy and her family. Of course, she would have loved to be in Africa with her parents and to see her baby sister, but when she thought of Mia and how miserable she was in her dad's house, she whispered a 'thank you' to God for all the good things in her life.

In no time at all, Sophie was back and ready to take her to the hairdresser's. Sandy and her brothers stayed in the kitchen with their dad and began to prepare for the party. Once Matty had gone, he asked them all to sit around the table.

'I wanted to have a little time with you on your own,' he explained. 'I need to talk to my children.'

As their dad said this, the boys winked knowingly at each other, but Sandy felt a little shiver of apprehension go down her spine.

'You know that you are the most important people in my life and I would never knowingly do anything to hurt you. But you must have guessed that I have become very fond of Sophie, and she of me. After your dear mother died, I never thought I could feel that sort of love again, and never looked to remarry. When I first met Sophie it was at a church function, and I thought what a bubbly, fun-loving girl she was. As I got to know her, I didn't think she would look at me—someone much older who was the father of three wonderful children—but she seemed to enjoy my company. She made me realize how lonely and empty my life was, especially in term-time when you weren't at home.

'Now we've become really fond of each other, and I would like to ask her to be my wife. However, I will not do that unless I also have your blessing. Sophie will never take your mother's place. She would not try to do that. She would not be a mother to you, but she could be like a big sister and a real friend.'

Mr Thompson looked at his children. The boys were grinning and winking, and saying to each other, 'I told you so!' Sandy looked very thoughtful.

'Dad, we guessed what was happening,' said Jack, 'and Philip and I have talked about the possibility of you marrying again. We just want you to be happy and certainly not lonely. Soon I'll be going to university, and it won't be long before Philip does too. As far as we're concerned, we like Sophie, and so long as we don't have to call her "stepmother", we're happy for you!'

Philip nodded his agreement. He was rather shy when it came to speeches, especially on the subject of love and marriage!

Sandy looked at her dad. 'I've been worrying about this ever since Christmas, when I realized you and Sophie were in love. I can't say I was very happy about it, but I did talk to Matty one day when she found me upset. We've prayed together about it. If I'm honest, I was feeling jealous that she might come between us. I'm sorry for that, Daddy. Now I've grown to like Sophie and I want you to be happy.'

Sandy was crying a little and went and put her arms around her dad.

'No one can ever take your place, Sandy, nor the place in my heart that I have for you boys. Each one of you has a special place, but I still have room to love Sophie. Do you understand that?' he asked his children.

They all nodded.

'Then is that settled?' Mr Thompson asked. 'Can I ask Sophie to marry me and know that my children will welcome her into the family?'

'Yes, Dad,' they chorused.

'Good! Then let's get on with the party preparations! It's going to be a wonderful celebration tonight!' he added.

10 The new term begins

Matty enjoyed her visit to the hairdresser's. It made her feel very grown-up to have her hair trimmed, washed and blow-dried. Then her nails were manicured. Sophie had hers done, too.

'You will be the belle of the ball tonight,' Sophie teased Matty. 'And so you should be on your birthday!'

By the time they returned to the farmhouse, it had been decorated with balloons and streamers. All sorts of party food were on the table. Matty was overwhelmed that Sandy's family had gone to so much trouble! Of course, they were having a party before the new term started, too. She began to understand that this family loved any excuse to celebrate! Sandy took her aside and Matty learned that there could also well be another reason to celebrate soon! Matty asked Sandy how she now felt about the possibility of her father marrying Sophie, and she was relieved to hear that Sandy was much happier about the idea than she had been after Christmas.

'I really like Sophie,' remarked Matty. 'She seems such fun, and more like a sister than a grown-up. I love the way she calls you Beatrice, and rolls her "r"s!'

'I'm glad she's chosen to call me that. It somehow shows me that she isn't trying to be my mum, but rather a friend,' replied Sandy.

'I wonder how Mia's doing. She really has a horrible time with her stepmother,' said Matty.

'I wish things could work out for her. It must be awful to have your mum leave you, and then have a stepmother who doesn't want you around,' commented Sandy. 'It makes me realize how well-off I am, because I know that Sophie loves me and wants to be my friend. It can't be easy for her to have a ready-made grown-up family!'

The party was a great success! Philip insisted they all play hide-and-seek, just in case Matty thought she was now too grown-up for the game! It was getting too dark to play outside, but there were plenty of places where the children could hide indoors, as the farmhouse was old and rambling. Jack was the seeker and it took him ages to find everyone! Finally, Mr Thompson said that they really had to think about going to bed, as they had the long journey back to school to make the next day. However, before they all retired, he wanted to make an important announcement.

'I have asked Sophie if she will marry me, and she has agreed!' he told them all.

Sophie was standing by him, and he put his arm around her waist.

'I am such a proud and happy man, with this lovely lady who is willing to marry me and my wonderful children all around me this evening!'

Sophie smiled, and everyone clapped and shouted 'hurrah!'

The children then disappeared, leaving Mr Thompson to put a ring on his fiancée's finger.

The next day, they were all up early and soon on their way back to London. Matty couldn't say enough 'thank you's to her friends. They had given her a wonderful Easter holiday and birthday. They had supported her through the most difficult days when her mum and baby sister both looked liked dying, and they had taught her more about her Friend and Saviour, Jesus. Other than at home in Burundi, there wasn't a nicer place she could have spent the holiday!

'Any time your family can spare you, you are welcome to be with us,' said Mr Thompson. 'We have loved having you, and it's especially nice for Sandy to have another girl around!'

Sandy and Matty were the last of the dorm to arrive back. Everyone was eager to hear the news of the holidays. It was hard for Mia, though, because her holiday had not been much fun, while everyone else had so much to share. The best news of all was that of the birth of Neema and the recovery of Matty's mum, and also the engagement of Sandy's dad. When Matty told everyone this news, Mia went very quiet. Matty looked at her and thought how thin she looked. Was she ill, or was it just because she was so unhappy? Once she and Sandy had unpacked their cases, she suggested that the three of them go for a walk in the garden before supper. There was just about time. Matty would have loved to play hide-and-seek, but somehow she felt that Mia needed their friendship and perhaps could tell them what was wrong.

The three girls found a seat in a warm spot of the walled garden.

'You're very quiet, Mia—is something wrong?' Matty asked her.

'I'm sorry,' Mia answered. 'I should be so happy for you about your sister. I am really, but it's just that my stepmother also had her baby in the holidays. She had a little boy, and she and Dad have called him Paul. They are so besotted with him that they didn't even seem to notice that I was home for the holidays. Dad kept on saying how much he had always wanted a son. Gloria wouldn't let me hold Paul, even though I would have loved to have done that. I just spent the holiday helping with the housework or keeping out of everyone's way. I was longing to come back to school and see you two—at least I know you care about me.'

Mia was struggling not to cry. Sandy put her arm around Mia's shoulder. 'We do care very much about you, and you are our special friend,' she reassured Mia.

'I wish we could make things better for you,' said Matty. 'We do ask God in our prayer times to help with your situation.'

'But what can God do?' asked Mia. 'I find it hard to believe in him. My dad and stepmother don't care, and my mum abandoned me years ago. There must be something very horrible about me for them to do that.'

'Of course there isn't! You're a lovely person,' insisted Sandy firmly. 'You just live in a very difficult family. God does love you, and if you can learn to love him, you will have a heavenly Father who will always be there for you, no matter what.'

Mia gave a big sniff and wiped her nose. 'I'll keep coming to the Christian Union meetings with you and listen. Maybe one day I'll believe. You two are the nicest people I know, and if loving God has changed your lives so much, maybe he can change mine too,' she said thoughtfully.

At that moment the bell sounded, so the girls ran indoors to get ready for supper. They found their places in the refectory. Almost everyone had returned by now, and the hall was filled with chatter as news was exchanged. Chloe came over and told Mia and Matty that her research project about the school was almost finished. Maybe they would like to read it, as they had both helped so much? The girls said they would love to, so it was arranged that they would meet the next day after chapel to do so.

Matty noticed that Mia ate hardly any supper. 'Perhaps she's just upset about having told us about Paul,' she thought to herself.

Before bed, Matty talked to her dad on the phone. The news was still good. Her mum had been discharged from hospital and was staying in a nearby hotel so that she could go each day to be with Neema and feed her. Neema was still too weak to leave the hospital.

'We're trying to make plans for the future,' her dad was explaining. 'As Neema is such a small baby, it may not be the best thing to bring her back to Burundi. I may bring Mummy and your sister back to England for a while. Please pray that we'll know what is the best thing to do.'

'I will,' Matty assured him, 'and so will Sandy. I know that God will help you to make the right decision. Please give them both my love.'

'Mummy will talk to you tomorrow evening. She's at the hospital right now,' her dad explained.

'I can't wait to talk to her again!' Matty replied excitedly.

The next day at breakfast, Matty noticed that again Mia was eating hardly anything. 'No wonder she's so thin!' she thought.

As arranged, Mia and Matty met up with Chloe after chapel. It made the two girls feel very important to be shown Chloe's project about the school. It included photographs of the wall painting which Mia had uncovered and the garden plan which Matty had carefully drawn. Rebecca was there with Chloe too. Ever since the half-term when they had camped together, she had been very kind to Matty.

'Did you have a good holiday?' she asked Matty. Matty told her about her time in France with Sandy's family, and also about her baby sister, and how they had celebrated her birthday. Rebecca laughed when she heard that they had all played hide-and-seek. 'You may be twelve now, but make sure you still have lots of fun!' she said. 'Everyone made me grow up too soon and I missed playing ordinary games!' It made Matty think of Philip's remark about not being too old to play hide-and-seek. Part of her didn't want to grow up at all, but another part was excited about changing into a young lady! She had really enjoyed having her hair done with Sophie. Life seemed very complicated when you were twelve!

In the afternoon, Miss Grace asked her dorm if they would like to go to the beach and then have tea in her room. All six girls were really pleased. They loved Miss

83

Grace, who always tried to make their experience at boarding school as much fun as possible. Now that she had heard Miss Grace's secret story, Matty understood why she loved children so much and wanted to give to them what she was never able to give to her own twins. As they walked along the beach, Matty told Miss Grace all about her baby sister, Neema, and about how her name also meant "Grace" in Swahili. She told her what a miracle it was that both her mum and her sister were alive, and how everyone in Sandy's family had prayed.

'Can I tell the girls about this when we have our next Christian Union meeting?' Miss Grace asked.

'Oh yes, please do,' answered Matty. 'I've learnt how much prayer matters, and that God really does hear us and help us.'

Miss Grace had baked all sorts of treats for tea. It was like a party! Once again, Matty noticed that Mia didn't eat. She began to get really worried. Later in the evening, when they were alone and undressing for bed, Matty asked Mia if she felt ill. 'You've become so thin,' she commented.

'Thin!' said Mia. 'I'm anything but thin! I'm fat and ugly! If I was slim and pretty, everyone would love me!'

Matty was very troubled. How could Mia have lost so much weight in just two weeks? Maybe she had lost some before the holidays and she just hadn't noticed. Mia hadn't eaten a proper meal since they came back to school, yet she thought she was fat and ugly! How could she think that? Matty didn't want to talk behind her friend's back, but she felt she needed to talk about it to Sandy. Was it just her imagination that Mia was thin?

11 Mia's illness

Soon everybody was back in the swing of the new term. The summer term was always enjoyable because there were more opportunities to be outdoors. For Matty, it was great fun to learn new games like tennis and take part in athletics. She laughed to herself when she remembered that only a year before she had created such a fuss when she was told about having to go to boarding school! She had never imagined that she would enjoy it so much! She did sometimes think about her friends from primary school, and wondered how they were getting on at Springhead High. Her dad had said that she might be able to go home for half-term because it looked as if her mum and Neema would be back in England by then. That really was something to look forward to! She would be able to look up her old friends, too, which would be really nice.

Matty wondered if Mia could come home with her. She was still worried about her friend. Mia was so thin and always looked pale. Matty and Sandy had talked about the situation and prayed together, and one day they decided they had to talk to a grown-up. They chose Miss Grace because she was so kind and understanding, and they knew she used to be a doctor.

'We don't want to tell tales,' the girls explained, 'but we are really worried about Mia. She eats hardly anything at all and is so thin. She thinks she's fat and that's why her family don't want her around. She's so unhappy and often cries herself to sleep. Could she have anorexia?'

Miss Grace listened carefully to all that the girls told her. She too had noticed that Mia was pale and thin, but she had no idea that eating had become such a problem. The girls told her about her family situation and how they had been praying for God to work in it in some way. Mia had continued to go to the Christian Union meetings and had shown interest in the Christian message, but she had not yet become a Christian. It was hard for her to trust God, for almost everyone in her life had let her down. Miss Grace promised to talk to Matron and make sure that Mia was seen by the school's doctor.

Miss Grace was as good as her word. That very afternoon she talked to Matron, who was a plump, jolly lady loved by all the girls. In the evening, after supper, Matron appeared in the dorm.

'Right, girls,' she said, beaming at all six of them, 'I want to weigh and measure you all, and check your hair, feet and teeth! It seemed best to do it at bedtime when you are undressing anyway. Brush your teeth well—it makes them nicer to look at!' She laughed. 'Who would have my job, peering into mouths and looking between toes!'

The girls lined up and were duly examined. Matron made no comment about the measurements. She pretended it was just a routine check for them all. Then they went to bed as usual. However, Matron was alarmed when she discovered that Mia weighed only four stone two ounces. Her bones were almost sticking out of her skin because she was so thin. Right away, Matron called the doctor and asked him to visit the next day.

During the next morning, Miss Grace came into the maths class and asked Mia to come with her. She gently explained that Matron had been worried because she was underweight, and so Dr Jones had come to see her. Dr Jones was himself a father of two young girls in the junior school. He was always kind to the boarders and no one minded being treated by him. His examination confirmed that Mia needed to go to hospital and get specialist help. The poor girl looked so frightened. Miss Grace tried to comfort her and promised that she would bring her friends to visit her.

Of course, the school needed to inform Mia's dad and Gloria about how sick Mia was. Her dad seemed shocked and denied that she could be unhappy or have any problems at home.

When Miss Grace took Matty and Sandy to visit Mia, they found Mia in a single room in a unit for teenagers. A drip was feeding her through her arm, and she looked very small in the large hospital bed. She hardly answered her friends when they talked to her. After the visit, Miss Grace took the girls back to school and tried to explain to the whole dorm about anorexia. She told them that the recovery process might take a very long time, and that it was both a physical and a mental problem. Mia had not deliberately starved herself but she was driven by strong emotional currents that swept her along. Miss Grace thanked Matty and Sandy for noticing and reporting that Mia was not eating properly and was becoming very thin.

'To think I was a bit envious of her being so slim!' commented Florence Jo, patting her own rather chubby body. 'Poor Mia, I just thought she was a misery!'

'There are many things in her life which are sad and have made her miserable,' said Miss Grace. 'When she does come back to school she will need all the friends she can get. I know that this Year 7 dorm will support her.'

The five girls nodded. They all felt so sorry for Mia. Apparently, if she didn't begin to put on weight soon and then maintain it, she was even in danger of dying.

Each day, Matty and Sandy went with Miss Grace to visit Mia, usually after supper. She didn't seem to be making much progress. Her dad had also been to see her. The girls kept telling Mia how much they missed her, and they encouraged her to get well. Now she was being fed through her nose by a tube as well as the drip, and she was putting on a little weight.

One evening when Matty was reading her Bible, she came across a verse in Isaiah which excited her.

'Look,' she said to Sandy, 'this verse must have been written just for Mia!' She read out the words:

Can a mother forget the baby at her breast?
  and have no compassion on the child she has
    borne?
Though she may forget,
  I will not forget you!
See, I have engraved you on the palms of my hands.
                              (Isaiah 49:15)

'We must tell Mia that God has not forgotten her!'

Sandy agreed. Matty underlined the passage in her Bible, and Sandy wrote the text out on a card for Mia, putting it in a safe place ready to take when they visited Mia later that day.

The girls were excited about sharing the text with her, and Mia seemed to take some interest and respond when they told her that God would never leave her or forget her. They left the hand-written text on her bedside locker.

A few days later, Matty and Sandy were told that Mia was to be moved to a special unit where they looked after people with anorexia. The unit was in another town, so they would not be able to visit her so frequently. That made them sad, but they promised Mia that they would pray for her every day.

Meanwhile, the news from Africa was exciting: Neema was now strong enough and big enough to fly back to England! Matty's family were given permission to visit the school one weekend so that Matty could see her sister for the very first time. All her friends were pleased for her and hoped that they too would be able to see the baby they had been praying for. Once again, Miss Grace came up with a special plan. She decided to entertain the family in her sitting room and invite the rest of the dorm, plus Louise, Laura, Rebecca and Chloe, to see Neema there.

Matty found it hard to concentrate on lessons the week before her family came! It seemed the longest week of Matty's life! At last, Saturday afternoon arrived and Matty sat on a bench near the drive so that she could see when the car turned into the school gates. She was almost beside herself with excitement! Christmas had been such a long time ago, and she was longing for a hug from her mum and dad, as well as a cuddle with the baby.

And what a cute little baby Neema was! She didn't murmur when her big sister cuddled her, or even when a whole lot of other schoolgirls (and some staff!) kept peeping at her and cooing over her! Matty felt so happy to be able to see her parents again, and they were delighted to see how well their daughter was looking and that she was obviously very happy at the school.

All too soon it was time for the family to go back home. Matty's dad had to fly out to Burundi again in a day or so, having been given only a little time off to bring his wife and baby back to England. Before they left Miss Grace's room, Matty's dad said thank you to everyone who had prayed for his wife and daughter through the difficult time of the birth.

'I know that it's only because of your prayers that my wife and daughter survived. Through this difficult time we, too, have learnt to love and trust in God. We thank God for this school, where our other special daughter, Matty, has come to love God and has helped us to know him too.'

Miss Grace smiled at them all and offered to pray for them before they went away. The room became very quiet as she thanked God for all his goodness to them all. Everyone joined in with a loud 'Amen' at the end.

12 The discovery

By the time summer half-term arrived, Mia was beginning to respond to her therapy. Her two friends were taken to the special unit to visit her and, to their delight, found that she still had the piece of card with the verse written on it.

'I read it every day,' she told them, 'and then I talk a bit to God. I'm learning to trust him. I don't feel so desperate or alone now. I feel a calmness, even when the black thoughts come and I feel I hate myself. When that happens, I just keep thinking about Jesus and calling out to him until they go away. I've got to stay in this place until I reach seven stone in weight. I'm told it will take a few months.

'My dad visits sometimes,' Mia continued. 'He keeps saying he's sorry and telling me that he does care about me. He promises that things will be different when I come home. I hope they will be. He's also promised to try to find out where my mum is and to tell her about me. I know she may not want to know me, but something inside me so wants to know about her. I keep reading my verse, though, because even if she never wants me, I know that God does. I need to remember that. When I have to eat a meal, although I still get feelings of hating food, I try to say grace and thank God for it, and ask him to help me eat it. There's plenty of time to think in this place!'

Matty and Sandy couldn't remember Mia ever saying so much at one time, but they were thrilled at what she had shared. They left the hospital feeling that in time all would be well for Mia.

Matty was very excited because she was going home for half-term. It had been about nine months since she was last in her own bedroom, with her own things around her, or had played in her own garden or seen her old school friends. She was a little sorry that she could not invite the twins to come home with her, but she knew that her mum had enough to do, looking after her and Neema. She was still not as strong as she used to be before she got so ill.

It was a lovely week at home! The weather was warm and mostly dry, so Matty was able to spend a lot of time outdoors. She helped her mum tidy the garden and they ate their meals outdoors as much as possible. It was great fun helping to look after her little sister. She understood how hard it must have been for Mia when her stepmother refused to allow her to cuddle Paul. She loved even the baby smell of Neema, except when she had a dirty nappy! Neema was a contented baby who smiled and gurgled whenever Matty played with her.

Matty was also able to meet up with several of her friends from primary-school days. They had teased her when they heard she was going to a 'posh' boarding school, but when they found that she was just the same, cheerful girl, they got on just as well as if she hadn't gone away. In fact, they all wanted to hear about her new life at the school and her visit to Burundi. Several of them came to her house to see Neema. Matty's mum made a whole batch of cupcakes and home-made lemonade for them all.

The nicest part of each day came after Neema had been fed and put to bed. Then Matty and her mum had time to sit and talk together. There seemed to be so much to talk about, especially about God and Jesus. They read the Bible together and prayed before Matty went to bed. It made Matty very happy to know that her mum and dad had now become real Christians.

All too soon it was time to return to school. On her last evening at home, her mum talked to her about the school. Did Matty want to live at home and go to the local comprehensive next school year, or did she want to stay at St Anne's? She could choose because her mum and Neema were going to stay living in England for the last year of her dad's contract in Burundi. 'You don't have to make your mind up at once,' her mum said, 'but we need to know before the end of term.'

On the way back to school, all sorts of thoughts went through Matty's mind. She loved it at St Anne's, but if she lived at home she could be with her mum and sister all the time. She just didn't know what to choose.

During the second half of the summer term, the lovely weather continued, and at the weekends the boarders spent quite a lot of time on the beach. Matty loved swimming and rock-pooling. Sometimes, she and Sandy would spend time in the school garden, just as they had done when she had first come to St Anne's. She would still help Sandy with her drawing, but she didn't need so much help with French these days.

One Sunday afternoon, Sandy suggested that they play hide-and-seek again. They hadn't done that for ages! Matty remembered Philip telling her not to get too old to play, so she agreed. Sandy began to count and Matty ran quickly, trying to think of a hiding place which she hadn't used before. As she ran through the shrubbery, which was very thick with bushes, she suddenly tripped over. She thought that her foot must have caught a tree root, but when she looked she found that there was some hidden brickwork, which gave way as she touched it. Behind was some sort of tunnel, almost completely hidden by the bushes. That would be a marvellous hiding place! She shivered a little as it was very dark, but she crept inside anyway. Matty could see that it was bigger than she had first thought. She decided not to investigate any further until Sandy was with her. It was a bit scary to do it on your own!

Meanwhile, Sandy had been searching everywhere and was completely puzzled as to where Matty might have hidden, so she began to call out for her to give herself up. Matty decided to do this because she wanted to get a torch and explore the tunnel with Sandy.

When Matty appeared from the shrubbery, rather scratched and dirty, her friend was amazed when she learnt where she had hidden.

'We need to get a torch from the dorm,' said Matty. 'I want to explore further in the tunnel. You will come with me, won't you?' she asked Sandy.

'How exciting! Of course I'll come! You stay here and I'll go and get my torch,' Sandy replied.

'Please get mine as well,' said Matty. 'Mine's a wind-up one and it's under my pillow.'

Soon Sandy was back and the girls started to explore the tunnel. It was really quite narrow, and for some of the way they needed to go on their hands and knees. It was dark and there were spiders, and both girls were a little scared as it seemed spooky. After a while, the tunnel broadened out into a cave. The girls could stand up again. They shone their torches around.

'Look!' exclaimed Sandy. 'There are bats up near the roof!' The girls were not afraid, so they looked at the little creatures hanging from the roof of the cave. They also found some huge boulders. They looked like a table and a stool, and there was also a place hollowed out like a recess in the wall.

'I wonder if someone used this place to hide in!' Matty wondered aloud. 'Maybe a pirate or a smuggler!'

'It certainly looks as if these stones were put here for a purpose as a table and stool,' said Sandy. Matty was starting to get a horrible feeling that they might find a skeleton or other remains—shivers were going down her spine.

'Come on, Sandy, let's keep going and see where this new tunnel leads,' she said, pointing at the place where the tunnel continued out from the cave. 'Then we can get back out into the sunshine!'

So the girls set off down the new tunnel. They had to crouch again at first, but gradually it became a little easier to stand up, and they thought they must be getting near the sea because the floor was damp.

'I wonder if this leads to the sea?' said Sandy. 'But if so, we must be under the cliffs somewhere.'

Just then, Matty slipped on the wet floor. As she reached out to the wall of the tunnel to steady herself, something crumbled and gave way.

'Help!' she yelled, thinking the wall was going to collapse on her. Sandy quickly turned to help her friend and shone her torch on the wall. Matty ended up sitting on the ground.

'I think you've found a secret hiding place in the wall!' Sandy exclaimed. 'Get up, Matty, come and see!'

The girls shone their torches into the hole in the wall and saw a bundle inside. They could only just reach it, and as they got hold of it, all the sacking ripped away to reveal two metal objects. They were very old, but as the girls lifted them out of the hole they could clearly see that they were a plate and a drinking vessel of some kind.

'Maybe this is what the person living here used,' said Matty. 'They used to use metal plates and cups in the past.'

'I don't think these are ordinary ones,' replied Sandy. 'I've got a feeling that they're from the church. This one's like a cup that's used for communion.'

'Chloe told me that all sorts of valuable things disappeared when the monastery was ransacked by King Henry VIII's men!' recalled Matty. 'You know, in the dissolution, or whatever they called it. And I think the librarian said something about lost treasure from the Abbey!'

Now the girls were getting really excited and imagining all sorts of things. They completely forgot the time until Matty's torch lit up Sandy's watch.

'Goodness! It's gone supper time! We will be in trouble!' exclaimed Sandy.

It took them quite a while to scramble back up the tunnel, through the cave, through the smaller tunnel and out into the garden. They carried the treasure carefully with them.

'Where on earth have you two been?' they heard Miss Grace call out. 'We were getting worried about you! And look at the state of you both! You're filthy!'

'We're really sorry, Miss Grace, we completely forgot the time,' Sandy explained. 'We were playing hide-and-seek when Matty fell into a tunnel. We went to explore it, and we've found some treasure—at least, we think it must be treasure!'

Miss Grace knew Matty and Sandy well enough to know that they were telling the truth, so she smiled.

'Treasure, eh? Maybe! Anyway, I think you'd better both get a bath and some clean clothes, and then we'll get you some supper. Meanwhile, am I to be trusted with your treasure?'

Matty and Sandy handed over their precious objects and Miss Grace took them carefully.

'I'll take them to the head. She'll know if they're valuable,' Miss Grace said.

13 The story of Mia's mother

While Sandy and Matty were having supper, they told Miss Grace the whole story of their adventure in the tunnel. She listened carefully.

'I'm sure it must date back to the time of the abbey,' Miss Grace said. 'Can I get Chloe? She'll be very interested. I've given the headmistress the things you found, and she, too, thinks that they're significant. She'll get an expert to look at them tomorrow.'

'Of course we don't mind Chloe knowing!' said Matty. 'She may even want to put the story in her book.'

Chloe soon joined them and she was very excited to hear their news. She would have liked to go down the tunnel herself, but the headmistress was having it fenced off for safety reasons, at least until it had been investigated properly. Chloe told Matty and Sandy that historians thought that some treasures from the old abbey—a silver chalice and a special plate called a paten, which were both used for communion—had been stolen, but this discovery suggested that someone had simply hidden them in the tunnel. They would just have to be patient and wait until the archaeologists had visited.

After the adventure it was hard to settle down to normal classes and exams at school! They noticed some

people working at the site where they had found the
tunnel, but that area of the garden was now out of bounds
to the schoolgirls. Miss Grace promised to tell them when
there was any news. Some newspaper reporters with their
big cameras also came to the school, wanting to interview
Matty and Sandy, but the headmistress did not allow them
to do so. They took pictures of the tunnel and also of the
wall painting which Mia had discovered.

Meanwhile, things were still slowly improving for Mia.
Matty and Sandy wished they were able to visit her more
frequently, but it was part of the policy of her unit to limit
the number of visitors. One day, however, she had a very
unexpected visitor. It was her mum! The social worker
came first and talked to Mia, telling her that her mum had
been found and would like to come and see her. She would
only be allowed to visit if Mia wanted to see her.

Mia had all sorts of feelings—some of anger and hate,
and some of longing and curiosity. She really wanted
to see her mum, but she was so scared of being rejected
again. After a day or two of feeling very confused, she
decided to talk to God about it all. Mia had gradually
begun to pray through her illness and was now beginning
to understand that God really was a loving Father who
would never let her down.

'Father God,' she whispered in her heart, 'I don't know
what to do. All my life I've remembered the smell of my
mum and longed for her to come home, but now I'm so
scared. If she didn't love me then, she isn't going to do so
after all these years. I don't know if I can face that. But
if I don't take this chance, I'll never know. I hate her for

what she's done, but something in me wants to love her because she is my mum. What shall I do?'

No voice answered Mia, but she felt that her mind was calmer after she prayed. She even dropped off to sleep and dreamed that her mum held her in her arms. She woke up with a conviction that she should agree to see her mum.

The social worker was very kind and understanding. She arranged for her mum to visit one afternoon. Mia struggled to eat her lunch that day, and having eaten it, the anxiety made her throw it up almost immediately. She tried to read a book to take her mind off the visit, but that didn't really work.

Eventually, the social worker brought in her mum. They looked shyly at each other, neither knowing what to say. Mia was surprised that her mum looked so young and pretty in a cotton summer top over her jeans. She didn't look old enough to be her mother! Was there some mistake?

Her mum broke the silence. 'Mia, my own daughter, Mia! I've longed so much to see you all these years!' she exclaimed.

'Then why didn't you come? Why did you leave me? If you'd loved me you would have stayed with me!' Mia's words came out full of anger.

'If only you knew the pain of leaving you and that I have never stopped loving you! Every single day I think about you, but I thought it best for you not to know me.'

Mia was still angry, but she also wanted to know her mum's story. Her dad had always told her that her mum had run away with another man. Who was this man who had been more important than her husband and daughter?

'Tell me what happened and why you didn't come back,' Mia said, rather bitterly.

'It's a very long story, and another time I'll tell it all to you,' said her mum. 'For now, I'll give you the bare bones. It will be up to you to believe me or not. If you never want to see me again, I'll understand. At least I will have had today, and seen my own daughter and tried to explain. I'm not trying to excuse myself. I am very, very sorry for all the pain and hurt I caused everyone.

'I was very young when I met your father—only sixteen. Life at home had been pretty miserable, and I was flattered by this man who made me feel special. I allowed him to make love to me and before long I found 1 was pregnant. My parents were furious and threw me out, so I went to live with your father. We were married quietly in a registry office not long before you were born. You were the sweetest little baby and we both loved you very much. But I was so young that I had trouble getting you to feed and later eat solid food. You used to throw it back at me all the time! Your father came home from work to find a frustrated mother, a dirty house and, often, a crying baby. He became more and more fed up with me. I was a very inadequate mother, but there was no one to help me. I really loved you, but I didn't know how to cope with being a mother. My parents had told me never to come home again, so I had no one to ask.'

She looked at her daughter, who was listening intently. Some of Mia's anger was melting away as she thought of her mum trying to cope without anyone to help or advise.

'Then, one day,' continued her mum, 'a man came to the door selling pictures. I was just making coffee, so I allowed him to come in and show the pictures to me. I desperately needed someone to talk to. He seemed kind. I didn't buy any pictures, but he asked if he could come another day, and, stupid as I was, I said "Yes".

'Well, he came again and again, making me feel important and pretty. He lived in a caravan, painting pictures, along with a whole group of hippies. He got me taking drugs, which gave me highs and made me feel better about myself until the effects wore off. I ran away with him one day when I was high on drugs. I hardly knew what I was doing. I wanted to take you with me, but he wouldn't let me. Deep down, I knew that the hippie commune and drug scene were not right for my baby, and that you would be better off with your father.

'How I regret that day! Of course, at first it was exciting, and I was still only nineteen years old and quite pretty. Soon I was whisked off to another part of the country. We didn't ever stay long in any one place. Our lifestyle was wrong—full of drugs and sex and theft and lies and heavy music. So many times I wished I could start my life again. I thought of you every day, but I was afraid to run away, and afraid that your father wouldn't want me. Once I wrote to him and asked for a picture of you. We didn't have an address, only a box number, and the only communication I received from him was a letter from his solicitor asking for a divorce. I signed it. What else could I do?'

'Did you have any more children?' Mia interrupted her mum.

'No. I made sure of that. I was so sorry that I had left you, and I didn't want to risk hurting anyone else.

'I stayed in the hippie commune for several years, becoming more addicted to drugs, and more and more unhappy. Then, one day, we were in a small town and I noticed that the door of a church was open, so I crept inside. I thought it was the one place where nobody from the commune would look for me. It's very hard to leave a commune. You know too many secrets, as well as being hooked on drugs. I remember it being cool and dark inside the church, and strangely peaceful. I found a corner behind a thick curtain and, in my desperation, I prayed that if there was such a person as God, would he rescue me. Then I fell asleep. When I woke up it was dark. I was shivering and shaking from withdrawal symptoms. Drugs are terrible things, Mia. They creep inside your body promising nice feelings, but then they take over and are cruel, painful—even terrifying. I was having nightmares. I know I screamed out, but inside that church there was no one to hear, except perhaps the God I didn't really believe in. Finally, I fell asleep again and was woken up by a man in a black dress shaking me gently. When I saw him I thought that maybe I had died and gone to hell. He was old and his face quite severe, and he was all in black. I began to shake again. He sat down beside me on the floor and asked me who I was and why I was in the church.

'For some strange reason I felt I should tell him the truth, so I did. I told him that the hippies would be looking for me, but I felt safe in the church. He sat quietly for a while, not saying anything, then he suggested that we should leave the church by the back entrance and just walk through the churchyard to the vicarage. He promised that he would keep me safe. I later realized that he was the vicar. I was hungry and shaky and needed the bathroom, so I agreed. He and his wife sheltered me for over two weeks. Then he heard that the hippies had moved on. Meanwhile, I was in a very bad way because I had no drugs and my body was craving them. That kind couple put up with my swearing and screaming and bad temper. They fed me, found some clothes for me and even just sat with me through it all. They didn't say very much, at least not to me. I think they may have been talking to their God. Sometimes they sang, and I loved the songs they sang. They brought peace to my troubled mind and body.

'After the hippies had left the town, this couple asked me what I wanted to do. I told them all about my life. I knew I could trust them—they had not betrayed me to the hippies. I asked if I could stay a little while until the cravings for the drugs had completely gone and I could trust myself in the outside world. I really had no idea what I was going to do or where I would go. They said I could stay, but they also knew of a sanctuary, a safe house for people like me. If I went there, I could earn my keep by helping on the farm, and also have time and space to think what I wanted to do with my life.

'So that is what I did. I went to live on the farm with several other people who had also had problems in their lives. It wasn't easy, but I gradually adapted, and I got a social worker who helped me back to normal life. I had never had a career because I was only sixteen when I gave birth to you, so I began to study. I was then able to get a job outside the farm and later I lived in a cottage in the next village. At long last I felt I was a normal person again, nine years after I left you.

'I know I have no right to be part of your life now, but I just wanted you to know the truth. One day, maybe you will be able to forgive me.'

Mia was very quiet for a while. She was tired out by her mum's visit. She was so emotionally drained that she had no idea what to make of all that she'd heard.

'What should I call you?' she asked her mum. 'I don't feel I can call you "Mum" because I've grown up without one. Gloria's not "Mum" to me either. I think I would like to see you again, but I need to know what to call you.'

'Why don't you call me Minty?' her mum suggested. 'That was my nickname at school, because I loved mints! No one has called me that since I left school, so it could be your special name for me.'

'All right, Minty,' Mia responded. 'Thank you for coming to see me. There's so much to think about, but I'd like you to come again one day.'

Minty gently took her daughter's hand in hers. 'Thank you, Mia,' she said. 'Thank you for even seeing me and listening to me. Forgive me one day, if you can.'

After she had gone, the social worker came to see if Mia was all right. Mia nodded. She was shell-shocked by what she had heard and she needed time to process it all. But something inside her was singing. She did have a mum. And her mum had never forgotten her.

14 The term ends

For several days, the archaeologists and press were buzzing around the school. The tunnel was properly excavated and in the cave a skeleton was found. Matty and Sandy were very relieved that they had not found it! It was dated back to Tudor times, when the abbey had been ransacked. The archaeologists believed it to be the remains of a nun who had escaped with the treasure—for the cup and plate were indeed the missing silver chalice and paten. Both had engravings which dated back to the thirteenth century. They were taken to the British Museum for examination and display. Chloe had quite a bit more to add to her book!

The restoration of the wall painting continued; it was going to be available for the public to see during the school summer holidays. There would be a charge for entry and this money would be used for more restoration work. Chloe's book was also going to be on sale to help raise funds for the school. Chloe was pleased because St Anne's had been her home, and although she was moving on to university to study English, she was sad to leave the school where she had been so happy. Rebecca was hoping to get a place in the same university and they wanted to share a flat. They had both worked very hard at their A levels and just hoped that their results would be good enough. This last year at school had been very important for both of them because they had now both come to faith in God and knew that they would not be facing the big, wide world on their own.

The first few days after finding the tunnel, Matty and Sandy had been treated like heroes, but both of them were glad when life settled down to normal again. The summer holidays were quickly drawing near, and Matty had a big decision to make about her future. Should she stay at St Anne's or go to live back home with her mum and attend Springhead High with her old friends? Matty wasn't bothered about Springhead High any more, but she would love to be back at home and see her little sister grow up. She began to ask God when she prayed each evening to help her to make the right choice.

Sandy was full of excitement. In the summer holidays she would be bridesmaid at the wedding of her dad and Sophie! Having worked through her anger and jealousy the previous term and holidays, she was now very happy for her dad and she accepted that Sophie would be like a big sister and not a 'wicked stepmother' to her. Matty had been invited to the wedding too, and her parents had promised to take her there. After the wedding, Matty's family would fly out to Burundi for a month, taking Sandy with them while her dad and Sophie had their honeymoon. Sandy's brothers were going to their grandparents and then to a summer camp. It looked as if it would be a wonderful summer holiday! Now it was Sandy's turn to have lots of injections ready to go to Africa! She didn't mind—she was so excited! At the end of the holidays they planned to meet up in Nairobi with Laura and Louise and have a day sightseeing in Kenya's great capital city.

The girls in the dorm were planning a midnight feast to celebrate the end of term. Polly, Rosie and Florence Jo had not been to the unit to see Mia, but they all said that they would like to. It had been a shock to them all to find that one of their dorm-mates had become so unhappy and then so sick. They asked Miss Grace if they could all go to visit Mia. At first she was hesitant, but then she decided to call the doctors at the unit and see how they felt.

'Hmm—five of them?' asked the doctor. 'I don't see why not. Mia is making good progress now. It might help prepare her for coming back to school.'

So it was arranged that one Saturday the whole dorm would go over. They decided among themselves that they would take their 'midnight feast' with them, even though it would then become an afternoon feast. They wanted to include Mia.

'What do you think?' Polly asked Miss Grace about the midnight feast.

'I think it's a great idea, but don't keep offering food to Mia. She may not want to eat in front of you yet. Remember, that is her illness—it's not that she's just picky.'

The girls hadn't thought of that and were glad Miss Grace had reminded them. They didn't want to make things harder for Mia. They all missed her.

'I really hope she's back with us next term,' stated Florence Jo. 'I hope we all stay together until we leave school!'

'So do I,' said Rosie, always the quiet one in the dorm. 'This year has been such fun, and we're so glad you came to join us, Matty!'

Matty went a little quiet. She didn't want to leave her dorm-mates, either. And then there was Miss Grace. She was more of a friend than a school official. She had helped Matty give her heart and life to Jesus, and that was the most wonderful thing that had ever happened to her. She knew that Miss Grace was to be housemistress to both Year 7 and Year 8 next year, as both years had only a few boarders.

Before the whole dorm went to see Mia, Miss Grace took just Sandy and Matty over one evening. They were able to sit in the unit's garden and chat. First of all, the girls told Mia about their adventure in the tunnel, and how the painting she had discovered was being restored.

Then, suddenly, Mia began to tell them all about her mum's visit and what had happened since she left home. Mia had seen Minty once again since that first time, and it had been a good meeting. She had also been seeing her dad each week and had talked to him about her mum. He knew some of the story and was glad that contact had been made. So Mia asked her mum to come regularly, and they had begun to talk about their lives. They even almost had some 'mother and daughter' times together. Minty herself was now back in touch with her own parents and asked Mia if one day she could bring them—Mia's grandparents—to meet her. Mia thought she would like that. Her dad's parents were dead, so she had no other grandparents.

'But there was one problem,' explained Mia. 'Could I forgive my mum for deserting me? I felt it was too much to ask, but all the time I kept the resentment inside me, I found myself getting dark thoughts again and I felt sick at the sight of food. The anorexia monster was getting to me again. Then I remembered when I spoilt your painting, Matty. I hated you and wanted to hurt you, but you forgave me and even tried to make friends with me. When I asked you why, you told me that you had thought about Miss Grace's story of how she forgave the killer of her husband and babies, and that helped you to choose to forgive. I remember you saying that you *chose* to forgive. I realized that I, too, had a choice. I could forgive Minty, even though what she did to me was terrible, or I could choose to hold on to my resentment and maybe be sick for ever. So I have chosen to forgive her. I know it will be a long haul back to health—the therapists have told me that. I know it will take a long time to really trust Minty and learn to love her, but I'm praying for God's help. Matty, please will you help me next term? I want to follow Jesus too, and I've asked for his forgiveness. I can only win this battle with anorexia if you all support me.'

'It's my turn now to make a decision,' thought Matty. 'Why did Mia ask me to support her, and not Sandy? Is this God speaking to me?'

After a few minutes of thinking quietly, Matty turned to Mia.

'Of course I shall help you next term, and each term until we leave school!' she answered.

Her decision had been made. She would stay at St Anne's. She would still see her sister every six weeks in the holidays, and maybe on visiting weekends too. A great peace filled her heart. She knew that she had made the right choice.

The end of term 'midnight feast' with all the dorm was a great success. The food was just put out for the girls to help themselves, and everyone was delighted to see Mia eat a little. They all told her how much she was missed, and to please get well enough to be back for Year 8!

All the parents arrived on the morning of the last day of term. They came to assembly and the headmistress spoke to everyone about the school year. The highlights were not only academic, she said, but also the discovery of what had so long been the secret of the abbey garden.

'We need to thank two Year 7 students for that,' she added. 'Matilda Morris and Beatrice Thompson, who were not too old to play hide-and-seek!'

Everyone laughed and clapped. Even Neema, sitting on her mother's lap, seemed to enjoy the joke!

About Day One:

Day One's threefold commitment:

~ To be faithful to the Bible, God's inerrant, infallible Word;

~ To be relevant to our modern generation;

~ To be excellent in our publication standards.

I continue to be thankful for the publications of Day One. They are biblical; they have sound theology; and they are relative to the issues at hand. The material is condensed and manageable while, at the same time, being complete—a challenging balance to find. We are happy in our ministry to make use of these excellent publications.

JOHN MACARTHUR, PASTOR-TEACHER,
GRACE COMMUNITY CHURCH, CALIFORNIA

It is a great encouragement to see Day One making such excellent progress. Their publications are always biblical, accessible and attractively produced, with no compromise on quality. Long may their progress continue and increase!
JOHN BLANCHARD, AUTHOR, EVANGELIST AND APOLOGIST

Visit our web site for more information and to request a free catalogue of our books.

In the UK: www.dayone.co.uk

In North America: www.dayonebookstore.com